Magnolia Mansion

Mysteries

Garden Girls
Cozy Mystery Series Book 6

Hope Callaghan

http://hopecallaghan.com
Copyright © 2015
All rights reserved.

Visit my website for new releases and special offers: http://hopecallaghan.com

A special **thank you** to **Wanda Downs** for taking the time to read and review *Magnolia Mansion Mysteries* and offering all of the helpful advice!

D1301882

Table of Contents

"Honor your father and your mother, so that you may live long in the land the Lord your God is giving you." Exodus 20: 12 NIV

Chapter 1

The long, sleek limousine coasted through the front gate of 122 Magnolia Lane and turned onto the gravel drive leading to the front entrance. When the car rolled to a stop, a tall, thin man dressed in a crisp, navy blue uniform climbed out of the driver's side of the car. He strode around the back of the limo and over to the rear passenger door in a few short steps.

He leaned forward and pulled open the rear door. A white-gloved hand appeared. The driver grasped the tips of the glove and out emerged a meticulously dressed, perfectly-coiffed woman with long blonde hair.

She stepped onto the gravel drive and made her way to the edge of the manicured lawn as she waited for the vehicle's final occupant to emerge. The driver jerked upright and stood at attention while a barrel-chested man with a short, thick neck and clump of dark brown hair stepped out of the vehicle.

A mischievous grin tugged at the corner of the driver's mouth as he watched the man adjust the cheap swath of carpet atop his head and then yank on the bottom of his worn, polyester jacket. With the flick of his wrist, he adjusted the black bowtie around his neck, cleared his throat and nodded at the driver.

The gentleman and his female companion strolled under the covered porch as they made their way to the front door. The woman's mouth dropped open as she stared at the lion's head knocker that covered a good portion of Andrea Malone's front door. The man paused for just a fraction of a second before grasping the round, metal ring and giving it two sharp raps.

Moments later, the door swung open and Andrea popped her head through the open door.

The stiff expression on the man's face melted and turned into a gentle smile. David Thornton opened his arms and his daughter, Andrea, stepped inside. "Daddy!"

Libby Thornton watched the exchange for a moment, waiting for her turn. Andrea released her grip on her father and reached for her mother. "Mom! I've missed you both so much!"

Pierce, the limo driver, removed his black cap and wiped the perspiration from his brow as he watched the exchange. He closed the passenger side door.

Andrea peeked around the side of her mother. "Pierce, is that you?"

Pierce swung the door shut, turned to face Andrea and grinned. With long strides, he

3

covered the distance between them, focusing his attention on one of his favorite people in the entire world. Pierce hadn't seen Andrea for over a year now. The last time he'd seen her was when she made a quick trip to New York. Right after her snake-of-a-husband, Daniel Malone, was murdered.

Andrea didn't wait for a reply. She sidestepped her parents and met Pierce on edge of the porch. She wrapped her arms around his muscular frame and laid her head on his chest. He closed his eyes and leaned his cheek on the top of the familiar blonde head. "His" Andrea's head. He blinked back the tears as he hugged the woman who had always been like a daughter to him. "It's nice to see you again, Miss Andrea."

Andrea tilted her head back. Her eyes widened as she studied Pierce. "I've missed you, Pierce. You're staying here with us." It wasn't a question. She wanted Pierce to stay. He was family. Her family.

Pierce turned to his employers, Mr. and Mrs. Thornton. David Thornton shrugged. "I'll leave that up to Andrea."

Andrea nodded firmly and marched over to the trunk of the limo. "Great! Pop the top!" Her hand smacked the top of the trunk. "Let's get this luggage in the house."

Pierce stuck a hand out. "Miss Andrea. You know I can't let you do that."

Andrea swatted at his hand. "Now, you know, Pierce," she mimicked his voice, "you can't stop me."

Pierce knew when he'd been beat. If Andrea wanted to do something, Pierce would not stop her. Even now, the girl had him wrapped around her little finger. Just like she had when she'd been just a bit of a thing running around the cold, sterile Manhattan apartment.

The Thorntons made no attempt to stop Andrea, either. She was headstrong. Always had been. Probably always would be. They watched as Pierce and Andrea lifted the luggage from the trunk of the limo and dragged it toward the house.

Andrea stopped at the front door and waved her parents inside. "After you!"

Libby Thornton crossed the threshold first as she stepped into the front foyer. Her husband was right behind her. They took a few quick steps inside and stopped to survey the large, magnificent entryway.

Andrea's mother spun around in a circle. She nodded her approval. "The pictures you sent us didn't do this place justice," she decided.

Her father shoved his hands in his pocket, his gaze focusing on the large living room and massive fireplace. "You live here all alone?"

"Well - not all alone," Andrea said. Brutus, her black lab, made an appearance as he rounded the corner of the butler's pantry and padded over to the group. She leaned down and patted his head. "This is Brutus."

Pierce leaned forward to pet the dog while Andrea's parents took a step back. Animals were not their cup of tea. They had lived in high-rise Manhattan apartments their entire lives. Pets took up too much time and energy in their opinion.

Libby's eyes narrowed. She waved her hands. "This creature - he lives here? Inside the house?"

Andrea stifled a giggle. She knew exactly what her mother was thinking; that dogs carried all kinds of diseases and were unsanitary. No. Her mother was definitely not a pet lover. When she was young, she had begged for a pet. Anything – a cat, a dog. Even fish. All to no avail.

But now her parents were in her house. Maybe being around Brutus would change their minds and they would realize that animals could be wonderful companions. Sometimes better companions than humans.

"Here, let me show you to your rooms."
Andrea grabbed the handle of the nearest bag
and began tugging it up the massive staircase.
Pierce followed behind, while Andrea's parents
brought up the rear.

The home had plenty of space for guests. The
guest wing boasted five bedrooms and three of
them had private baths, while the other two had
an adjoining or "jack-and-jill" bath.

Andrea had decided to give both her parents
and Pierce the rooms with private baths. At the
center landing, halfway up, Andrea turned right
and headed up the remainder of the steps.

Andrea stopped at the first door on the right.
She turned the knob and opened the door. "This
room is for Pierce," she told them.

Pierce pushed his luggage through the
doorway and stepped inside. The room had
masculine touches. There was a smoky gray
bedspread and matching gray curtains. A deep,
cherry wood dresser faced the large, king-size

bed and a small armoire sat in the corner. On the other side of the armoire was a six-panel wooden door that led to the bath.

Pierce wandered over to the door and glanced inside. To the right of the door was a white pedestal sink. To the left - the toilet. Across from the toilet, tucked away in the corner, was a large, stand-up shower.

Andrea followed him into the bedroom. She ran her hand down the corner bedpost. "I hope this room is okay," she fretted.

Pierce put an arm around Andrea's shoulder. He grinned, flashing a set of pearly-white teeth. "This is perfect, Miss Andrea," he assured her.

Andrea left Pierce to unpack and led her parents down the hallway to the double doors at the end of the hall. She didn't miss the limp in her father's step. "Is your foot still bothering you?" The three of them glanced down at his feet. His pants, a good three inches too short, revealed a pair of mismatched socks. One was black, the other dark green.

Andrea's eyes traveled upwards as she studied his suit – a suit that looked very familiar. It was a suit that her father had had for as long as she could remember. She reached out and flicked the tip of the tattered lapel. "How old is this thing?"

Andrea's father was the biggest penny pincher on the planet. Not that he needed to be. David Thornton was a successful stockbroker on Wall Street and her mother, a neurosurgeon. Her mother was a bit of a spendthrift so his thriftiness evened them out.

Libby crossed her arms and shook her head. "You know your father."

Andrea didn't answer. Instead, she rolled her eyes and started walking again. *Quirky. Her parents were just a bit quirky*, she reminded herself.

At the end of the hall, Andrea opened the doors leading to the room her parents would occupy. She had secretly nicknamed the room, "The Queen's Quarters." It was the nicest bedroom in the house. Other than her own, of course. The room was spacious. A large, king-size bed filled an entire wall. An ornate canopy covered the top. Tucked in the corner was a small writing desk and padded high-back chair. The antique wooden desk overlooked the garden and side yard.

Inside the bedroom was a matching set of armoires. Both were a great deal larger than the one in Pierce's room. Her mother slowly nodded as she studied the room. Andrea let out a sigh, relieved that the bedroom met her exacting standards.

On the other side of the room was the entrance to the bath. A large, granite countertop and double sinks covered one wall. A brand new glass shower with a deep soaking tub sat next to it. Off in the corner was a small walk-in closet, the perfect size for her parents.

Her mother squeezed past Andrea and stepped inside the bathroom. She reached inside her purse and pulled out a travel packet of Lysol wipes. She peeled the sticky cover off and plucked one out.

With wet wipe in hand, she walked over to the nearest faucet and began to wipe the handles.

"You don't need to do that," Andrea assured her.

Her mother paused, for just a fraction of a second, and then continued wiping. "One can never be too careful, Andrea."

David reached around his wife and snatched the wipe from her hand. He crumpled it up and tossed it in the nearby trash can. "If Andrea said this place is clean, it's clean."

Libby Thornton gave her husband a dark look before she plucked a second wipe from the pack.

She stepped over to the other sink and began wiping.

Andrea's shoulders sagged. She let out an exaggerated sigh. "Mother! These sinks are brand new! No one has ever used them." She waved her hand around the room. "Everything in this room is new, right down to the handle on the toilet."

Her mother shook her head and continued to wipe. "Well, you can never be too careful. After all, day laborers installed these sinks." She sniffed. "Heaven only knows what kinds of germs were on their hands."

Andrea groaned inwardly. Arguing with her mother was futile. Andrea was convinced her mother had some kind of obsessive-compulsive disorder when it came to cleanliness. There was no sense in trying to talk her out of it. She had no idea how her mother had made it through medical school, let alone treated her patients!

She gave her father a quick hug, reaching up to adjust the toupee on his head that had shifted and was now just a tad off-kilter. "I'll be in the kitchen if you need me."

Andrea looked at her mother one last time. She and her wet wipes had moved on to the cabinet drawer pulls.

Andrea and Brutus stopped by Pierce's room on their way downstairs. She peeked in through the open door. He was inside, hanging his shirts in the armoire. "Everything up to snuff?" she teased.

Pierce paused. "I feel like I'm on vacation," he admitted. He hooked the hanger on the rod and turned around. "This is a big house for just you, Andrea."

Andrea nodded. She'd been thinking about that. That the house was big for just her. She glanced down the hall in the direction of her parent's room before she stepped inside Pierce's room and closed the door behind her.

Pierce had always been one of Andrea's closest confidantes. She could tell him things she wouldn't dream of telling her parents. "I've been thinking about that." She lowered her voice. "What do you think if I were to open a bed and breakfast? You know, with paying guests."

Pierce shoved his hands in his front pockets and rocked back on his heels. The house would be perfect for that type of business – but for her to take it on all by herself? He wasn't so sure about that.

He opened his mouth to speak. Andrea answered the question she knew was coming. "Of course, I'd have to hire someone to help me run it."

He grinned and nodded. "Then it might work."

She reached for the doorknob and paused. "How's Alice?" Alice was her parent's full-time housekeeper and part-time cook. She'd been a part of the family for almost as long as Pierce.

Alice, like Pierce, held a special place in Andrea's heart.

Pierce grabbed a shirt and slipped it over the hangar. "That woman is as feisty as ever!"

Andrea grinned. Alice *was* feisty. Her parents had hired the ball of fire (as Pierce liked to call her) when Andrea was just a baby. She was tough on the outside but like melted chocolate on the inside. Especially when it came to Andrea.

Andrea and Brutus headed down the steps. She glanced out the window above the front doors, her eyes resting on the large metal dumpster off to the side. The sight of the dumpster reminded her that she needed to retrieve one of the old gaslights from the dumpster before the trash company picked it up the next morning. One of the workers had accidentally tossed the light in the bin and later admitted to Andrea that he had mistakenly thrown it out.

She and Brutus wound their way down the final few steps and headed outdoors. The large, green bin was just inside the fence, close to the road. She grabbed the top of the bin and hoisted herself up on the narrow edge. She leaned over the side to have a peek. Luckily, the light was at the top of the heap.

With a quick glance back at the house, Andrea pulled herself up and over the side. She landed inside the cavernous box with a dull *thud*. She grabbed the side of the bin to steady herself as she scanned the inside. It was bigger than it looked!

She bent down to grab the light when she heard the sound of car tires as they crunched on the gravel drive. Andrea lifted her head and peered over the top of the bin. It was her friend, Gloria.

Gloria coasted into the drive and pulled her car in behind Andrea's. She climbed out of the car, her gaze focused on the sleek, shiny limo.

Gloria had never seen a limo up close and never in the small town of Belhaven. Then she remembered that Andrea's parents, who recently retired, were coming to town. *Funny, Andrea had never mentioned they rode around in a limo*, she thought to herself.

She shoved the car door shut and headed for the front door when she heard a small voice call out "Over here!"

Gloria swung her head around. There was no one there. She shrugged and took another step toward the front porch when she heard a dog bark. *Woof!* It was Brutus. He was standing near the fence, not far from the dumpster.

She heard the small voice again. "Hey! I'm over here!"

Gloria lifted her gaze. The voice was coming from the dumpster. She made her way over to Brutus and bent down to pat his head. "When did you start learning to talk?"

"Gloria, it's me! I'm in the dumpster!"

A slender hand with manicured nails popped up from inside the container.

Gloria stood upright and stared at the bin. "Andrea?" She made her way over to the edge. "What on earth are you doing in a dumpster?"

The hand disappeared, only to pop up seconds later. This time it was holding a small, antique wall light. "Can you grab this?"

Gloria pulled herself onto the side of the bin and reached for the light in Andrea's hand. She set it on the ground nearby then pulled herself back up. She twisted her head to peer over the edge.

Andrea was in sight now, standing just on the other side of the bin.

"My goodness. How on earth did you get in there?" She looked around. "Better yet, how are you going to get out?"

Andrea scrunched her brows together. She hadn't thought about that. She tucked a stray strand of blonde hair behind her ear. "Good question..."

"I'll go grab the ladder from the shed," Gloria said. She took one hand off the bin when something inside caught her eye. "Hey! What's that?"

Andrea looked behind her. A large chunk of paneling sat squarely in the center of the bin. It was a piece of wood paneling that had been on Andrea's kitchen wall.

Andrea squatted down and leaned forward. She grasped the edge and pulled it forward for closer inspection. Taped to the back side was a painting.

She grabbed both sides of the paneling and held it up. The painting was of a woman with long, flowing dark hair. On top of her head was a bonnet. A large, black feather fanned the top of her hat. Tied around the woman's chin was a long, white scarf that held the hat in place.

The painting was the top half of the woman's body. She was wearing some sort of dark green dress. Draped over the top of the dress was a shawl. The shawl was the exact same color as the woman's hat.

Gloria leaned in for a closer inspection. The woman in the painting was quite young. She had to have been in her mid-to-late 20's. Her expression was solemn, but her bright blue eyes twinkled with mischief.

Andrea turned to Gloria. Her forehead crinkled. "This was part of my old kitchen wall." Andrea had just had an entire wall removed between her kitchen and a small hallway that separated the kitchen from the library next door. A beautiful, marble bar area and barstools replaced the old paneled wall.

Andrea handed the piece of paneling to Gloria, who carefully laid it on the ground next to the gas light. "Let me go grab the ladder."

She turned around just in time to see a tall, dark figure emerge from the rear of the house. It was a man dressed in some sort of uniform. Gloria remembered Andrea mentioning her parent's butler or driver. His name was on the tip of her tongue. *Eric, Derick....*

The man stepped over to Gloria. He thrust his hand out. "You must be the infamous Gloria," he said.

Gloria put her hand in his. "And you must be...."

"Pierce," he offered. "Pierce Wright."

Andrea's head bobbed up and down from inside the dumpster. "Uh, can you do that later?"

Gloria let go of his hand. "Oh my gosh! I almost forgot about Andrea!"

She dashed over to the shed in the far corner of the yard and plucked the ladder from the peg, just inside the door.

Pierce was hovering over the side of the dumpster when Gloria returned. He took the ladder from Gloria, then hoisted it over the top and propped it against the inside wall.

He pointed into the bin. *"What is that?"*

Gloria stepped on the small ledge next to Pierce and peered into the dumpster. He was still pointing. There, beneath a pile of wood paneling and some old 2x4's was what looked to be a human hand - or what was left of a hand. More like protruding bones or quite possibly fingers.

Andrea followed their gaze. Her eyes widened in horror. She stumbled back and flattened her frame against the side of the bin. Her hand flew to her chest. "Holy smokes!" she gasped.

She scrambled up the ladder and jumped over the side, landing with a *thunk* on the manicured lawn below. She jumped to her feet and brushed the dirt and debris from her pants. "I-I think there's someone in there."

Gloria glanced back to make sure Andrea hadn't been injured in the fall before scooching along the edge of the metal bin for a closer look. *Yes, it was most definitely a hand*, she decided.

Pierce pulled up beside Gloria and focused his attention on the inside. "Now what?"

Gloria gave Pierce a hard look. "We call the police."

Chapter 2

Officer Joe Nelson joined them on the edge of the dumpster and peered in. He kept one hand on his gun and flung his other hand over the side to steady himself. The muscle in Officer Nelson's jaw tightened. He turned to Gloria. "Did you touch anything?"

Gloria's eyes slid to Andrea. While they were waiting for the police, they had moved the chunk of wood paneling and the painting inside. Gloria wasn't 100% certain what they had done could be construed as tampering with police evidence. After all, no one had technically touched the body...

Still, to err on the side of caution and make sure they wouldn't be labeled as suspects, she decided it was best if she told Officer Joe about the painting.

"Well, there was one other thing. It's inside the house," she explained.

Joe nodded. "You wanna show me what you got?"

"Follow me," Andrea said. Joe Nelson followed her in the front door. Gloria and Pierce brought up the rear.

Andrea's parents were nowhere in sight. *They must still be somewhere around here,* Gloria thought.

Andrea pointed to the wall light. "I crawled into the dumpster to get that," she told him truthfully. "The workers accidentally threw it away."

Joe Nelson pointed to the painting. "You found that in the dumpster, too?"

Andrea nodded.

"The crime lab will want to take a look at this." He reached for the painting and looked up at

Gloria. "I'm sure you're itching to find out what this is."

Gloria nodded.

He went on. "Course, it's not against the law for you to take a couple pictures of it."

Gloria's eyebrows shot up. *Why hadn't she thought of that?*

Andrea pulled her phone from her rear pocket. She turned it on and switched the screen to camera. She bent down and snapped a couple photos. "The light isn't very good right here."

Gloria picked up the piece of paneling and held it at an angle so that the light from the open front door shined down on it.

Andrea nodded. "Much better." She snapped a few more photos.

A movement outside the front door caught Gloria's attention. The crime scene van was pulling in the drive. She started to set the painting against the wall when Andrea stopped her. "Wait!" She leaned in, her face mere inches from the edge. "There's something here in the corner!"

Gloria leaned over for a closer look but everything was blurry. She didn't have her glasses on and couldn't see what Andrea was talking about - but Pierce did. "Oh, yeah! I see it too!"

Andrea turned her phone back on and got a close-up shot of the corner.

The two investigators were out of the vehicle and heading for the front door. Officer Joe met them in the drive. Gloria was right behind him. She had every intention of finding out what was inside that dumpster!

The two men were covered head-to-toe in white. Their uniforms were white. On their feet were white foot coverings. They each pulled on a pair of white gloves as they walked. "Whatcha' got Joe?" one of them asked.

Joe explained the situation as they made their way to the dumpster. "Yeah, the property owner was in the dumpster trying to get an old light that the construction workers accidentally tossed out. When she moved some stuff to the side, she saw what appeared to be a human hand – or the skeletal remains of one," he added.

The two male investigators nodded. One of them pulled his tall frame up and over the edge of the container while the other investigator hovered on the outer edge.

The one inside the bin reached down and picked up a broken sheet of paneling lying on top of the pile. He set it off to the side. Below that was another board. He moved that board to the side and reached for the next. With each board he moved, he revealed a bit more of a hand. When all of the boards were out of the way, an arm was clearly visible.

Gloria's heart thumped in her chest, growing louder with each piece of paneling the investigator moved. It was as if she was watching one of those archaeological digs on TV, except this wasn't dirt – it was trash!

The investigator continued his slow, methodical task as he removed every little bit of debris from the center of the bin. It wasn't long before an entire skeleton was completely exposed.

Gloria frowned down at the remains. *Why hadn't the construction crew noticed it when they filled the dumpster?* she wondered.

Could it be that someone had placed the skeleton inside the dumpster *after* the workers were done? The thought hadn't occurred to her until that exact moment.

Wouldn't at least some of the bones be broken if trash had been tossed on top of the fragile skeleton?

When the entire skeleton was unearthed, the worker inside the dumpster removed a glove. He reached inside his pocket and pulled out a camera to take pictures.

The investigator on the outside did the same as he moved to different spots around the dumpster. Next, he took pictures of the outside of the bin, the yard, the house. Everything.

The second investigator slipped his camera back inside his pocket and walked back to the van. He pulled the side door open. He reached inside and pulled out a large, plastic bag and a long, narrow stretcher. He carried the stretcher and the bag back to the dumpster and handed the bag to the investigator still on the inside.

The man opened the bag and carefully slid the skeleton inside, starting from the skull and working his way down.

When the bones were in the bag, the investigator slid the long, thin stretcher under the bag. The remains must not have weighed much because he easily lifted the stretcher over his head and slid it across the top edge of the dumpster.

The second investigator grabbed the stretcher and carried it to the back of the van, where he carefully laid it inside.

The investigator inside the dumpster took a few more photos of the spot where the body had lain before he began to sift through the rest of the trash, searching for clues.

Gloria began to sweat. Not so much from the excitement of the investigation, but from the heat. There were few clouds in the sky and the sun was scorching hot as it beat down on her. Beads of sweat clung to her brow. She wiped them off with the back of her hand.

Pierce, who was right next to Gloria, pulled on the front of his damp shirt as he tried to fan his body. "Man, it sure is hot out here."

Finally, the second investigator was satisfied there was nothing else in the bin. He climbed out, using the ladder that Gloria had pulled from the shed.

Officer Joe was waiting under a nearby shade tree.

The investigator removed the white cap that covered his head and nodded to the bin. "That all you got?"

Joe shook his head. He signaled the man inside. "There is one more thing..."

The men walked inside the front door and turned to the side. Propped on the wall, near the front door, was the painting. "This was on top of the pile," Joe told the man.

The investigator nodded. He lifted the sheet of paneling and headed for the door.

Andrea's shoulders sagged.

"We'll return this after the lab is done examining it," the man promised.

Andrea watched the investigators and Officer Nelson climb into their vehicles and back out of the drive. With one last look of longing, she quietly closed the door.

Gloria could hear murmured voices coming from somewhere in the living room.

"My parents," Andrea mumbled under her breath. "Come meet them."

Gloria followed Andrea into the living room. She lifted a brow at the sight of Andrea's parents. Whatever she thought Andrea's parents would look like – this was definitely not it.

Andrea waved her hand to the couple seated on the edge of the sofa. "Gloria, these are my parents, David and Libby Thornton."

Gloria stepped forward. "I am so pleased to finally get to meet you both." She extended her hand to Andrea's mother first. The woman stared at it but made no move to grasp it.

Finally, she took Gloria's hand in a limp grip. She quickly released it and then wiped her hand on the front of her black slacks.

Gloria stiffened her back as she watched her wipe. *Does this lady think I have cooties?*

She did a small mental shake of her head and turned her attention to Andrea's father. Her eyes were drawn to his ill-fitting polyester suit, which was at least two sizes too small. Gripped in his jaw was a thick stogie. He plucked the cigar from his perched lips and extended his hand.

His grip was firm and warm but his eyes were cold and calculating. Gloria's stomach lurched as he scrutinized her. She felt as if she were some sort of fascinating bug he was studying under a microscope.

Gloria swallowed hard and looked away. Andrea wasn't kidding when she said her parents were different.

The uncomfortable moment passed when Andrea turned to her parents. "Would you like a tour of the house?"

Without waiting for an answer, she headed to the front foyer and started up the stairs. Gloria was familiar with Andrea's home so she skipped the tour and waited for them on the first floor.

The upstairs tour didn't take long, and soon the three were back where they began. At the bottom of the stairs, they made a left and headed through the dining room, past the butler's pantry and into the kitchen.

Andrea's mother, Libby, stepped over to the kitchen sink and gazed out the window at the flowering gardens and rear yard. "You've done a lovely job on the house, Andrea."

"Do you really think so?" It was obvious Andrea craved her parents' approval.

Her father added his two cents. "It can't hurt the resale value."

Gloria frowned. She wasn't sure if she cared for him. He was not what Gloria had expected.

Pierce put his arm around Andrea's shoulder. "The home is beautiful, Andrea." Gloria crossed her arms. Now *that* was more like what a father should say. Maybe she had the two mixed up and Pierce was really Andrea's father.

They stepped into the library for a quick look around before heading down the small hall that connected the back of the house with the front entrance. Tucked away in the corner was a door that led to a small powder room. In the small hall, directly beneath the stairs was another door. One that Gloria had never noticed before. "What's in here, Andrea?"

Andrea tilted her head as she warily eyed the closed door. "That leads to the basement."

Gloria lifted a brow. "That's interesting."

Andrea shivered and rubbed the goosebumps that had popped up on the sides of her arms.

"Actually, I've never been down there," she confessed.

Gloria's interest was piqued. She took a step closer. "And why not, dear?"

Andrea recognized the familiar look. The look that said: *I know there's more to this story than what you're telling me.*

"It's kind of spooky. I've made it down a few steps to take a quick peek, but that was all. It gives me the willies."

Gloria decided she *really* had to see what was down there. She squeezed by Andrea's father and grabbed the doorknob. "I'm going to have a peek myself if you don't mind."

Andrea recognized the look of determination on Gloria's face that said she was going to go down there whether Andrea wanted to or not. Andrea nodded and took a small step back.

Gloria twisted the vintage glass door handle and pulled. The door creaked open with a low moan that almost sounded like someone saying "no." For a fraction of a second, Gloria paused. She gave herself a mental shake and took her first step down.

With her right hand, she grabbed the handrail. With the other, she groped the side of the wall until her hand made contact with a light switch. She flipped the switch and a small, bare bulb illuminated the stairwell.

She took a second step down. It creaked almost as loud as the door itself.

Pierce watched Gloria from the top step. "I'll go with you," he offered.

Gloria turned; a small smile of gratitude covered her face. She was more than a tad relieved she wouldn't be the only one going down.

Andrea's parents, on the other hand, didn't make a move. It was obvious they had no interest in checking out the basement. Not that

Gloria was surprised, especially that her mother wouldn't go down.

Andrea chewed the bottom of her lip and watched Pierce and Gloria's descent. She was torn. If she ever wanted to see what was down there, now was the time! "I guess I'll go, too," she relented.

The steps were narrow and steep. At one point, Pierce had to duck his head to avoid whacking it on the slanted ceiling.

At the bottom of the stairs, the trio stopped. The room was dark. The air was damp and cool.

Gloria blinked, giving her eyes a few moments to adjust to the lack of light as she gazed around.

A bit of light beamed through a small, square window. Just enough for Gloria to spy a bare bulb hanging from the rafters.

She cautiously stepped over to the bulb and pulled on the string hanging next to it. Light flooded the dark, cramped space.

Now that the light was on, the first thing Gloria noticed was the dirt floor. Her eyes moved from the floor to the walls. The thick walls consisted of large fieldstones, cemented together.

Big, round metal pipes hung down from the ceiling. On one wall was a rusty, metal cabinet tilting at an awkward angle. It was empty except for a few old glass jars and a cardboard box.

On the other wall, next to the small window, was a set of cement steps. The steps led to a set of double doors. It was an outside entrance into the basement!

Gloria tiptoed over to the stairs and started up. "I never noticed these before."

Andrea shrugged. "I knew they were there. I figured they led to the basement but I've never tried opening them."

When Gloria got to the top, she stuck a hand on each door and pushed. The doors easily lifted and swung open. Gloria looked behind her. "Andrea, these aren't even locked!"

Andrea and Pierce followed Gloria up the steps and out of the basement. The three of them stood out on the back lawn and stared down at the open cellar doors. "Anyone could sneak into your house!"

Andrea tilted her head and studied the doors. "I-I guess I never thought about it."

"We're going to put a lock on this today!" Gloria told her.

Pierce agreed. "We most certainly are!"

They made their way back down the steps and into the basement. Pierce was the last one down. He closed the double doors behind them.

They headed back across the musty basement and in the direction of the main staircase. When they rounded the side, Gloria spotted something else. It was a small, round door tucked back in the corner. She had almost missed it.

She stepped over to the door and kneeled down. The door wasn't very big. Just large enough to wiggle through if someone really wanted to.

Her gaze zeroed in on the metal handle and a round lock that hung on the front. It reminded Gloria of a combination lock. This one was red and rusty, and instead of a combination, there was a key hole in the center.

Gloria grabbed hold of the lock. It was heavy in her hand - like solid lead. She pulled down but the lock refused to budge.

Andrea peeked over her shoulder. "I wonder what's in there."

Gloria dropped the lock. "You still have your phone? I want to take a picture of this."

Andrea pulled her cell phone from her back pocket and turned it on. She handed it to Gloria. "Just press the screen."

Gloria leaned in and snapped a couple pictures of the front of the lock. She turned the lock over and rubbed her finger across the back. There was something etched on the back but she didn't have her glasses on and the print was too small. She snapped a picture and handed the phone to Andrea. "Can you send those to me?"

Andrea nodded as she reached for the camera. She pressed the screen a few times and looked up. "Okay, you should have them."

Gloria gazed one final time at the lock before she stood up and brushed the dirt from her knees. "Did the workers come down here?"

Andrea nodded. "A couple times to, you know, to work on the mechanical stuff."

Gloria stuck her hands on her hips. She was dying to know what was inside. She made a mental note to look for something that might pick that lock.

Andrea's father hollered down the steps. "Are you done down there?"

Andrea glanced up to the top. "We're on our way."

Andrea led the way up the steps, followed by Gloria. Pierce brought up the rear.

Her mother peered at Andrea. "Your father and I were just wondering…what was going on outside in that – that dumpster-thingy?" she asked.

Andrea and Pierce exchanged uneasy glances. They knew Andrea's parents well enough to know they would not like what they were about to hear.

Andrea took a deep breath and blurted out. "There was a human skeleton in the dumpster." She squeezed her eyes shut; waiting for what she knew was coming next.

Her father exploded. *"A human skeleton! Good heavens above!"*

Andrea raised her hands, as if to calm her parents. "We're not sure where it came from or how it got there." She hoped the explanation would help. Maybe just a little.

Without saying a word, her mother turned on her heel and headed down the hallway. Her high heels clicked sharply on the marble floor. Moments later, they could hear the creak of the steps as she headed to the second floor.

Gloria tried to help. "The fact that the remains were skeletal means the person wasn't recently deceased," she theorized.

Andrea's father peered at Gloria through his dark-framed glasses. "I am fully aware of that."

Andrea's mother returned moments later, wearing a surgical mask and a pair of white surgical gloves.

Andrea lifted her hand to her lips. *"Mother!"*

Even Andrea's father seemed surprised. "Now Libby, don't you think you're carrying this germaphobe thing a little too far?"

Libby's eyes narrowed over the rim of the mask. She ignored her husband's comments as she faced her daughter. "Lord only knows what's hidden inside these old walls. For all we know, there could be more bodies!"

Gloria frowned. She couldn't argue with that. The woman had a point. She remembered watching the show, *"If Walls Could Talk"* and grinned in spite of herself, certain that if these walls could talk, they'd have a lot to say!

Gloria glanced at her watch. "I better get going."

Andrea walked her to the door. "The skeleton in the dumpster has me freaked out. This is the second body we found now," she pointed out. "Maybe this place is haunted and I should sell it and move somewhere else." She glanced back at her parents. "They're convinced I should move back to New York."

Gloria gave Andrea a quick hug. "That's up to you, dear. No one should make that decision but you."

On the way to the car, she whispered a small prayer for Andrea and for her safety. And patience with her parents. The poor thing had her hands full!

Chapter 3

Mally was waiting at the kitchen door when she got back to the farm. Gloria absentmindedly patted her head.

She wondered about the painting they had found. Gloria knew as much about art as she did the stock market, which was nothing. Nada. Zip. The fact that the painting had been hidden behind the wall – and that it hadn't been damaged when the crew took the wall down – was interesting.

She tried to think back on the history of the old place. What she'd heard over the years. It wasn't much. The old couple that had lived there for years had died long ago. Whoever inherited the house had never bothered to come to Belhaven. Not even once. The fact that the owners sold the place without ever checking it out always struck Gloria as odd.

The previous owners had left behind a house full of antiques, some worth a pretty penny. The mystery of the mansion was growing by the day. And what *was* behind that small, locked door in the basement?

She pulled her glasses from her purse and headed to the dining room and her computer desk in the corner. Andrea had forwarded the pictures to Gloria's home email and texted them to her phone.

She plopped down in the chair and turned her computer on. She opened her mail and pulled the pictures up on the screen. With a couple quick clicks of the keyboard, she had a full screen shot of the painting.

As she studied the picture, a thought occurred to her. If Andrea never bothered to go down to the basement, she wondered if she had ever gone into the attic. Gloria decided to ask her about it the next time she talked to Andrea.

Things had been a bit slow around the small town of Belhaven lately. The last big excitement they'd had was when Ruth had been under investigation for a county-wide drug ring operation.

Thankfully, investigators had cleared Ruth of any wrongdoing and she was now happily back to work down at the post office. During the investigation, Ruth had been staying at Gloria's house, so solving that mystery had been a double blessing. Ruth was back to work and Gloria had her house to herself again.

Which reminded her that she needed to call her boyfriend, Paul. Officer Paul Kennedy. He had his own houseguests at the moment. His son, Jeff, and daughter-in-law, Tina.

Gloria fingers flew over the keyboard as she typed in a description of the woman with the solemn expression and mischievous eyes. She did several different searches but nothing even remotely close to the painting popped up.

Her stomach grumbled loudly. She glanced at the clock on the screen. It was past lunchtime!

She eased out of the chair and headed back to the kitchen. Mally, and her cat, Puddles, knew what time it was and they were patiently waiting by the kitchen pantry for Gloria to feed them.

After she filled their food dishes, she wandered over to the fridge and peered inside. It had been several days since she'd gone to the grocery store and it was slim pickings inside the fridge. There wasn't even a pack of lunch meat.

Gloria made a spur-of-the-moment decision to head down to Dot's Restaurant. There was no way her stomach would make it to the grocery store and back before eating.

Dot's Restaurant was the only restaurant in the small town of Belhaven and Gloria's friend, Dot Jenkins, and Dot's husband, Ray, owned it.

Gloria grabbed her keys off the hook, her purse off the chair and headed out the door.

The drive into town took just a few short minutes. She passed by the Palmer's farm on her way into town. Gloria wondered how they were doing these days. Their son, Seth, had gotten in serious trouble with the law recently.

Gloria eased into the open parking spot facing the front of the restaurant. The place was busy and she could see her friend Dot's head dart back and forth between tables. Dot caught her eye as she walked in the door and wandered over to an empty table for two in the corner. She pulled out a chair and started to sit down when she spotted her best friend, Lucy, who waved her over.

Gloria zigzagged around several tables and plopped down in the seat across from her. She eyed the two items on Lucy's lunch plate: a hamburger and a piece of chocolate pie.

She glanced at the coffee mug nearby. Gloria pointed to the cup. "You still on that hot-chocolate-only kick?"

Lucy's red head bobbed up and down. "Yeah! Believe it or not, I've lost ten pounds since I switched over."

Gloria dropped her purse on the floor and shook her head. How could a person add *more* sweets and chocolate to their diet and still lose weight?

Dot made her way over with a fresh pot of coffee and a cup. She set the cup on the table and poured. "So what's going on over at Andrea's place? Margaret said Officer Joe and a crime scene van were parked in the drive."

Gloria sipped the coffee and glanced at Dot over the rim of the cup. "You're not going to believe this."

She went on to tell the girls about the dumpster and the skeleton. She started to give them the lowdown on Andrea's parents but stopped short. That would be a lot like gossiping and although sometimes it was hard, she tried her best not to gossip. They would meet

Andrea's parents soon enough and could form their own opinion, she decided.

Lucy picked up the ceramic teapot and poured hot water into her empty mug. She tore the edge of the hot chocolate packet and dumped the powdery mixture inside. She grabbed a spoon and started to stir. "You have a picture of the painting?"

Gloria nodded. She fumbled around inside her purse and then pulled out her phone. She turned on the screen and scrolled to the picture. She handed the phone to Lucy. Dot peered over her shoulder as they stared at the snapshot. "Wow! That's just crazy!"

Lucy looked up. "And this was stuck to the back of a sheet of paneling they took down inside Andrea's house?"

"In her kitchen." Gloria took another sip of coffee. "There are a lot of secrets inside that old place."

She turned to Dot. "Who here in town might know something about the Johnsons?"

Dot set the pot on the edge of the table and stared out the window thoughtfully. "Hmm. You know, Eleanor Whittaker might remember something about them."

Gloria snapped her fingers. "You're right! Why didn't I think of her?"

Eleanor Whittaker had lived in Belhaven all her life. All 90+ years of it. She lived a block away from Lake Terrace, not far from Margaret and Don Hansen.

Gloria wasn't sure exactly how old Eleanor was, but remembered a few years back when the town had thrown a surprise 90th birthday party for her down at the VFW hall. Gloria hadn't seen her in quite a while, but the last time she had, the woman was smart as a whip – her mind like a steel trap.

Lucy dipped her finger in the swirl of whipped cream on top of her chocolate pie and stuck it in her mouth. "There is someone else."

Gloria was all-ears. "Who?"

"Doc Decker."

"That's right," Dot agreed. "If anyone knows the history and residents of Belhaven, it would be Doc Decker." Doc had owned the town's pharmacy, *Main Street Medicines,* for decades. He and his wife, Martha, had retired years ago. The town had gone without a pharmacy until Brian Sellers came along and opened it back up.

Gloria added the Deckers to her mental list. "You have an extra notepad back there I can borrow?"

"I'll bring one back with the food," Dot told her. "By the way, I'm guessing you came here to eat..."

Gloria had almost forgotten the reason she was there. "I'm starving," she admitted.

Gloria knew Dot's menu by heart so she didn't bother looking at it. "I'll have a bowl of chili." She eyed Lucy's half-eaten burger. "And a cheeseburger."

Lucy and Gloria had almost finished their lunch when Andrea and her parents walked through the front door. Andrea's mother was still wearing the surgical mask and gloves. Her father wore the same stony expression on his face - the old stogie still firmly clenched between his teeth.

The diners smiled and nodded at Andrea. Andrea's mother, Libby, got more than a few sideways glances. The looks didn't seem to bother Andrea. Somehow, Gloria knew Andrea was accustomed to the odd stares. Her mother probably wore a mask out in public quite often. She wondered if perhaps the poor woman didn't have some sort of serious phobia.

Gloria carried her check to the cash register. Dot glanced over Gloria's shoulder in Andrea's direction. "Would you get a load of Andrea's mom?"

Gloria nodded. "She seems a bit – uh – overly-cautious about germs."

Dot shook her head as she took Gloria's money. "No kidding."

Lucy wandered over to pay her bill. "So what's up with the mask? Does she think we all have some sort of deadly virus or something?"

Gloria shrugged. Poor Andrea. If it wasn't one thing, it was another. In between dead bodies and odd parents, Andrea seemed to have a black cloud hanging over her head. Of course, one would never know it. She was always so upbeat and happy. Most of the time.

Gloria looked over at Andrea's glum face. She sure didn't look happy at the moment.

Gloria wound her way 'round the tables and stopped in front of their booth. She gave Andrea's shoulder an encouraging squeeze.

Andrea smiled up at her but the smile didn't reach her eyes. She looked like she was being tortured. Gloria leaned down and whispered in her ear, "Call me later, dear."

Libby turned her attention to Gloria. "This place does meet minimum health code standards, I assume." The mask moved up and down as she talked.

Gloria sighed. "Yes, Mrs. Thornton. It most certainly does."

Dot was at the table now. Gloria said her goodbyes and headed for the door. It was Dot's turn to deal with them.

Gloria climbed into her car and headed toward the lake. Her first stop: Eleanor Whittaker's place.

Chapter 4

Gloria pulled into Eleanor's circular drive. Before she could change her mind, she opened the driver's side door and slid out. The drive was long and wound its way through the front yard. Gurgling nearby was a stack of wooden barrels. Water ran down the center of the basins and drained into a small pool surrounding it.

Lining the sidewalk, leading to the front steps, was an array of pink hydrangeas and multi-colored begonias. Gloria climbed the steps to the front door. She reached out to ring the doorbell when the door swung open.

Eleanor Whittaker appeared behind the screen door and gazed out. "Gloria Rutherford."

Gloria smiled at Eleanor's floral housecoat. It was white and dotted with pink roses. Small, pearl buttons ran down the center. There was an embroidered pocket on each side. On one pocket was a bluebird. On the other, a bright, yellow sun.

"I hope I'm not bothering you," Gloria apologized.

Eleanor fumbled with the handle, her hands shaking ever-so-slightly. "No. Come in. Come in."

Gloria squeezed through the opening and stepped into the living room.

Eleanor grabbed her metal walker and started across the orange shag carpeting, in the direction of the kitchen. Gloria hadn't been in Eleanor's house for decades. She glanced around. It looked the same as it had all those years ago. Down to the arrangement of the furniture.

She made a mental note to see if perhaps Eleanor wasn't at a point where she could use a little handyman work around the house. The church had volunteers for that and Gloria was certain they wouldn't mind adding Eleanor to their list.

The walker shuffled across the carpet then scraped hard against the kitchen linoleum floor. "Would you like a cup of tea?"

Gloria shook her head. "No thanks."

Eleanor pushed the walker off to the side and pulled out a kitchen chair. "Would you like to sit down?"

Gloria nodded and pulled out a chair. She settled in and watched as Eleanor eased into the seat beside her. "I hear you're a bit of a celebrity these days." Eleanor peered at her through her wire-rimmed glasses. "Sounds quite exciting."

Gloria smiled. "It is. In fact, that's why I'm here."

Eleanor's eyes lit up. She leaned in. "Really?"

"What do you know about the last couple who lived in the old Johnson mansion?"

Eleanor gazed past Gloria and out the rear window. "You mean the big house on the hill that someone just bought and fixed up?"

"Yep."

Gloria had very vague memories of the couple. She remembered one time when she was young; she'd been walking by the house, on her way down to the lake to visit one of her friends.

The old man had been out in his drive. She could feel a pair of eyes on her as she walked by the creepy place. She turned to glance towards the house when she noticed him standing there. He was watching her through the bars of the wrought iron gate. Glaring at her, really.

It scared the dickens out of her. When he took a step in her direction, she took off running as fast as her little legs would take her. She didn't stop running until she reached her friend's house. She made her mother pick her up later that day, too terrified to walk back by the house.

"Abe and Barbara Johnson. Those were the last ones to live there. Of course, before that Abe's parents had lived there." Eleanor rubbed her thumb over a small speck on the table. Her eyes clouded. "I don't recall their names, though."

Gloria grabbed her purse and pulled the pad of paper Dot had given her. She slipped on her reading glasses and started to jot down a few notes. She looked up. "Do you remember if they worked? If they had children?"

Eleanor nodded. "Abe. He worked down at the grain mill for years. Right up until he had that accident and one of his thumbs was severed in a wheel." She made a slicing motion across her thumb. "Cut it clean off."

She went on. "After that, he retired. Course he was into woodworking. Some sort of custom cabinetmaker."

Eleanor got up. "Sure you don't want some tea?"

Gloria shook her head. She waited as Eleanor fixed a cup of tea and sat back down. "What about his wife, Barbara?"

Eleanor sipped the tea. "She was a bit of an odd duck. Never really came out of that house, except for when the two of them would get in the car and go somewhere. They even had their groceries delivered to their door. Every Monday morning like clockwork."

Gloria remembered that part. She remembered her mother telling her a similar story. One time Gloria herself caught a glimpse of the deliveryman outside the front door, handing the bags to someone just out of sight.

"Do you remember anyone ever visiting them? Family? Children?" Gloria was curious.

Eleanor shook her head. "No. Not even once." She squished her eyes together thoughtfully. "I don't believe they ever had children." She shrugged. "At least not that I can remember."

It was Eleanor's turn to ask questions. "Did something happen over there at the place? Wasn't there a body found out back in the shed not long ago?"

Gloria nodded. "Yeah." She wasn't sure how much she should say. Eleanor wasn't the gossiping kind. At least not that Gloria knew of. Plus, everyone in town would find out what happened soon enough. "We found a human skeleton inside the dumpster out in front of the house earlier today."

Eleanor's eyes grew as round as saucers. Her hand flew to her throat. "You don't say!" She picked up her teacup. "They always said that place was haunted. That ghosts roamed around inside."

The place sure did seem to have a lot of odd occurrences and bodies. Gloria stood. "Thanks so much for talking to me, Eleanor. You've been very helpful."

Eleanor got to her feet. She grabbed her walker and followed Gloria to the door. "If I think of anything else, I'll give you a call," she promised.

"Thanks. I really appreciate that." Gloria paused. "You look good, Eleanor. I hope I'm half as healthy as you when I reach your age."

Eleanor tapped the side of her forehead. "Still sharp as a tack." She lowered her hand and opened the door. "The Lord blessed me with good health and I'll be here as long as He sees fit."

Gloria smiled. "Which is precisely how long any of us will be on this earth."

Eleanor watched Gloria climb into her car. She waved at her before closing the door.

Gloria pulled her notepad from her purse and grabbed a pen. "Wellness visits to Eleanor," she jotted down on the pad before slipping it back into her purse. Eleanor was a sweet lady and it would be a shame if anything happened to her.

Gloria headed up the hill and away from the lake. She couldn't decide if she wanted to head over to Doc Decker's place or wait to do that some other day.

She drove through town and at the last moment decided to stop in the post office to see if Ruth had heard anything. Gloria's friend, Ruth Carpenter, was head postmaster at the Belhaven post office. She was on top of all the happenings in town. Gloria was certain Ruth had heard all about the remains.

Gloria squeezed Anabelle into one of the tight parking spaces near the door and eased out of the driver's seat. The parking lot was half-full, but that didn't mean all of the people were inside the post office. A lot of them took care of their business inside and then headed across the street to run other errands or have lunch at Dot's Restaurant, which was directly across the street.

Gloria opened the front door and stepped inside the air-conditioned lobby. She was the only one in there besides Ruth.

Ruth whirled around when she heard the tinkle of the front door. When she saw who it was, she rushed over to the counter. "Did you hear about the body found in the dumpster at Andrea's place?"

Gloria nodded. "It wasn't really a body. Just a skeleton," she told her.

"How did you....?" Ruth's eyes narrowed. She slammed an open palm on the countertop. "Let me guess! You were there when they found it!"

Gloria walked over to the counter and set her purse on top. "Yep. We found it under a pile of old paneling. The stuff that Andrea took out of the kitchen."

Ruth raised an eyebrow. "Do they think the body was behind the wall?"

"It's a possibility," Gloria admitted. "After all, it was in with all the other stuff that came out of the kitchen."

Of course, the remains were intact. It was possible that someone had put it there, believing that no one would notice it. That it would be hauled away to a landfill and covered in tons of trash, never to be seen again.

Actually, the more she thought about it, the more that theory made sense. Of course, Gloria wasn't ruling anything out yet. There was still the possibility it *had* been behind the wall. Hidden away.

And then there was the painting, which was as much a mystery as the skeleton was. Last but not least, there was the small, locked area in Andrea's basement.

Gloria didn't mention the painting. "So is anyone talking? Any theories on who the body might belong to?"

Ruth shook her head. "All I've heard so far is," Ruth raised her index finger, "One. The place is haunted and should've been condemned years ago."

Gloria interrupted her. "Let me guess. Judith Arnett said that."

Ruth nodded. "Two. Andrea is cursed and dead people are following her around."

Gloria burst out laughing. That was ludicrous. She doubled over as gales of laughter took over. She finally stopped laughing and wiped the tears from the corners of her eyes. "That's a good one. Next they'll be saying I'm planting bodies just so I'll have a mystery to solve."

The smile disappeared from Ruth's face. She swallowed hard and studied the floor. Gloria stuck a hand on her hip. "Did someone say that?"

Ruth fiddled nervously with the ink blotter on the side of the counter. "Well..."

Gloria leaned in. "Who had the nerve to say such a thing?" It took a lot to get Gloria ticked, but when she did...Whoa! Watch out!

Ruth recognized that look! She clamped her lips tightly together and shook her head. There was no way she was going to set off 4th of July fireworks between Gloria and a certain unnamed party.

"You don't believe it, do you?" Gloria demanded.

Ruth stiffened her back. Her lips formed a thin line. "Of course not! If not for you, I'd be in prison right now!"

Gloria relaxed a little. "True." If not for that handy-dandy little spy camera Gloria had set up and caught Ruth's nemesis red-handed, she probably would be in prison..."

Ruth leaned forward. "Sour grapes, Gloria. Nothing but sour grapes. Remember that."

Ruth was right. Gloria glanced down at her watch. "I better head home. Let me know if you hear anything else," she added.

Ruth stopped her when she got to the door. "Hey! I heard Andrea's parents are in town and that her mom wore a surgical mask and gloves into Dot's."

Gloria opened the door. "Yeah. She's uhhhh.. different. Let's put it that way." She didn't wait for an answer before she stepped outside.

She stomped over to the car, a scowl on her face and her feathers still a bit ruffled by the idea that someone thought she was somehow responsible for coughing up dead bodies.

Gloria yanked the car door open and slid inside. *I guess that meant she was also responsible for the drug trafficking, not to mention bringing bank robbers to town....* she decided.

Gloria started Annabelle and headed towards home. When she pulled into her drive, her friend, Margaret, pulled in right behind her. Margaret was waiting on the sidewalk by the time Gloria finished parking the car in the garage. "I heard you found another body."

"Skeletal remains," Gloria corrected.

Margaret waved a hand dismissively. "Body. Skeleton. It's all the same," she said.

The two women wandered up the steps. Gloria turned the key in the lock and pushed the porch door open. "You want a glass of tea or lemonade?"

Margaret flopped down in the rocking chair on the porch. She dropped her purse on the floor next to her. "Sure. Bring me whatever. I'm not picky."

Gloria nodded and headed indoors. Mally was waiting in the kitchen, her tail thumping hard on the linoleum floor. Gloria opened the kitchen door. "Go say 'Hi' to Margaret," she told her.

Gloria pulled two glasses from the cupboard and slammed them on the counter. She wandered over to the freezer and grabbed a tray of ice cubes and pitcher of lemonade from the shelf. She was still stewing a bit about the comment Ruth had made.

After she put the lemonade back in the fridge, she carried the glasses to the porch. She handed one to Margaret before sliding into the chair beside her.

Margaret eyed her friend as she sipped the cool drink. "You look fit to be tied," she commented. The two had been friends for more years than either of them could count and Margaret knew Gloria well enough to see she was stewing.

"Someone told Ruth they thought I was creating mysteries for attention," she admitted.

Margaret snorted. "That's crazy! Where on earth would you find bodies?" She set the glass on the small table beside her. "Sounds like something Sally Keane would say." Sally worked part-time at the Quick Stop grocery on the corner of main street. She was also dating Officer Joe Nelson. Of course, *she* would already know about the remains in the dumpster!

Gloria's eyes narrowed. She never had been a huge fan of Sally's. Every time Gloria stopped in the grocery store, the woman moaned and carried on about something. Her feet hurt. She wasn't making enough money. The lights in the store were too bright. They made her eyes burn...

"Or it could be Patti Palmer. I heard she's not very happy with you these days."

Gloria hadn't thought about that. Yeah, Patti probably did hate her. Of course, it wasn't Gloria's fault that her son was a criminal.

Gloria popped out of the chair. She opened the kitchen door and reached inside to grab her cell phone from her purse. She slipped her glasses on and scrolled through the screen until she came to the picture that Andrea had taken of the painting.

She handed the phone to Margaret. "We found this stuck to one of the sheets of paneling that had been in Andrea's kitchen."

Margaret squinted at the picture on the screen. "This looks like an oil painting."

Gloria nodded. "You know anyone who might be able to take a look at it?" Margaret and her husband, Don, had an extensive art collection. "The police took the painting as evidence but Andrea should be getting it back soon."

Margaret handed the phone back. "I have a friend who's an art dealer in Grand Rapids. Let me know when she gets it back and we'll take a run down to his gallery."

Gloria set the phone on the small side table and grabbed her glass. "Thanks, Margaret. I had no idea where to even start with this..."

Margaret picked up her glass of lemonade and took a sip. "Aren't you wondering why I stopped by?"

Gloria nodded. Come to think of it, it *was* more than a little odd for Margaret to just "pop in" unexpectedly. "I talked to Liz earlier. She said David had left her a message, telling her that the judge was getting close to a decision on the coins."

The "coins" were coins that Margaret, Gloria's sister, Liz, their cousin, David, and she had found at her Aunt Ethel's farm in the Smoky Mountains. From everything they'd been told, the coins were worth a lot of money.

The government had filed a motion to take possession of the coins. Gloria's cousin, David, who also happened to be an attorney, was fighting them. If allowed to keep the coins, they would all become millionaires!

"Why didn't Liz call me?" she grumbled.

"She tried to," Margaret pointed out. "In fact, you probably have a message on your answering machine."

Gloria sighed. Her shoulders sagged. "I'm sorry. I don't know what's wrong with me today," she groaned.

If Gloria was honest with herself, she'd woken up on the wrong side of the bed, so to speak.

Margaret paused. Gloria was normally upbeat, happy-go-lucky, and ready to take on the world. "Is everything okay with Paul?"

Gloria shrugged. "Haven't heard from him lately. What with his kids living with him and all." Maybe that was it. Maybe she was just aggravated with the world and someone spreading rumors that she was "creating" mysteries was the last straw.

After Margaret left, Gloria wandered around the house aimlessly. Mally followed her from room-to-room. She glanced down at her dog. "Let's go for a walk!" Mally's tail thumped the wall. *Woof!* Mally loved walks!

Gloria grabbed her sweater off the hook near the door and stepped out onto the porch. She and Mally wandered down the sidewalk, past the garden and headed down the path that ran between the farm fields.

Soon, it would be harvest season and the dull hum of the tractors as they traveled back and forth across the fields would fill the air.

Fall was a beautiful time to live in Michigan. The changing color of the trees. The crisp, cool air. It was a welcome change from the muggy summer heat.

Her son, Eddie, had called the other night. He and his wife, Karen, lived in Chicago. They were planning an October color tour to Michigan and had asked Gloria if they could stay at the farm for a couple days. It was just the two of them.

Eddie and his wife had decided years ago that they didn't want children. Instead, they wanted to focus on their careers and each other. Gloria supported them in their decision but secretly wondered if someday they might not regret it.

Gloria's other son, Ben, lived in Houston with his wife, Kelly, and their twins, Ariel and Oliver. The family tried to come home every summer to visit, but for the second year in a row, the children were too busy. Instead, Ben promised they'd be home for the holidays.

If Gloria had to choose between a summertime visit and the holidays, she'd rather have them around for the holidays.

Last but not least was her daughter, Jill, and Jill's husband, Greg. They lived in nearby Green Springs with their two boys, Tyler and Ryan.

She and Mally headed in the direction of the woods and the creek that ran along the edge of the property. She shoved her hands in the pocket of her sweater as she walked. "What do you think about having Tyler and Ryan come spend the night?"

She reached down and patted Mally's head before she continued walking. She liked that idea. The last time the boys had stayed over had been right after Ruth's crisis and the yard sale. School would be starting soon and then they'd be too busy to spend time with her.

She decided to call her daughter when she got back in the house.

The two of them stepped into the woods and wandered over to the creek. There had been a lot of rain the last few weeks and the creek was overflowing. Mally didn't seem to mind. She wandered over to the water's edge and dipped her head to take a drink.

Gloria settled in on the log near the bank and reached down to pick up a leaf that had fallen. She twirled it between her fingers and studied the pattern. God's creation always left her in awe.

She wondered how Andrea was faring with her parents. She didn't want to judge them, but had to admit to herself they were a couple of odd ducks. At least Andrea had Pierce. He seemed like a nice guy. More like what Gloria had envisioned Andrea's father to be like.

Her mind wandered to the remains. She wondered whose they were. The investigator had put the body in the bag rather quickly, but from what she could see, it looked as if there was some kind of clothing still on the body.

She pushed herself off the fallen tree and brushed the dirt off her backside. She wandered over to the stream.

Had Andrea or Pierce noticed the clothing? she wondered.

Mally was back from her wanderings. Gloria reached over and tickled her ears. "You ready to walk back?"

She let Mally in the kitchen first, and then followed her inside. She found Puddles curled up on a kitchen chair. He lifted his head when he heard them come in. Gloria reached down and stroked his back. "I'd take you on our walks but I'm afraid you'd run off and I'd never be able to find you."

She hung her sweater on the hook and glanced over at the counter. The light on her answering machine was blinking. She pressed the button.

"Hi Gloria. It's Liz. I wanted to let you know David called. The court is getting close to making a decision. He said we should hear something in the next couple weeks."

She heard a muffled noise. Like Liz was covering the phone. "Look, I gotta go. Al's here." The message ended abruptly.

Gloria hit the "erase" button. Al. She must mean Al Dickerson. Gloria had played a bit of a matchmaker at her last get-together. A cookout. Liz and Al had hit it off. She was happy for Liz and happy for Al, whose wife had passed away a little over a year ago.

She frowned. Her own love life was in the tank. She remembered Margaret's words. Maybe she was cranky. And lonely.

She grabbed her cell phone. Before she could change her mind, she sent Paul a text message. "Lonely girlfriend, looking for a date. Please call if interested in helping."

She hit the "send" button before she changed her mind.

She set the phone on the table and headed to the living room. She made it as far as the dining room when the cell phone chirped. *Maybe it was Paul!*

She ran back into the kitchen and squinted at the screen. Her heart sank. It was Andrea. "Hello, dear."

"They're driving me crazy!" Andrea whispered. "Hang on." Gloria heard a commotion, as if Andrea was moving.

"Can I come over?" she begged.

Gloria grinned into the phone. "Yes, of course. I'm home."

"Great! I'll be right over." Gloria set the phone back on the table and shook her head. It made her wonder if maybe she didn't drive her own daughter, Jill, crazy!

Chapter 5

Andrea's sleek sports car pulled in the drive a few minutes later. Gloria chuckled under her breath. *Poor thing*, she muttered under her breath.

Gloria stepped onto the porch and waited for her young friend to emerge from the car. The look on Andrea's face said it all. She flopped down in the rocking chair, closed her eyes and leaned her head against the back. "I don't know if I'm going to survive this visit," she moaned.

Gloria settled into the chair next to her. She reached over and patted her hand. "Of course you are, dear." She paused. "At least they're not moving in with you. Permanently."

Andrea's head jerked up. Her eyes widened in horror. "Bite your tongue!"

Gloria laughed. "Are they really that bad?"

Andrea rubbed her chin. "You have no idea. My mother is looking for local exterminators to come fumigate the house. My dad is insisting I move back to New York."

She wrinkled her nose. "No daughter of mine is living in this little hick town. They probably don't even have a proper police force." She mimicked her father and did a pretty good job, at that.

Gloria pushed her foot on the floor and gave the rocker a gentle nudge. "What does Pierce think?"

Andrea let out a long sigh. "He thinks he should move in with me to protect me."

That didn't sound like such a bad idea. The fact that someone had been inside her house not long ago. And now discovering a dead body in her dumpster? That would give any parent reason to be concerned.

Gloria had an idea. "Have you thought about getting a roommate? After all, that is a big house."

Andrea stared blankly at the field and barn across the street. She had tossed the idea around a few times. But it would almost be like admitting defeat. Like she couldn't handle living on her own.

"Pierce mentioned that Alice is thinking about retiring. She's sick of living in the city," Andrea said.

Gloria nodded. Andrea had mentioned her parents' housekeeper, Alice, more than once. How she was like a second mother and had been with the family as long as Andrea could remember.

"What if Alice came here to live with you?"

Andrea's long, red fingernails tapped the armrest. She nodded. It was a thought. It would appease her parents. Pierce would be happy.

90

Gloria would be happy. She loved Alice dearly. It was an idea!

"I think I'll give her a call. Run it by her." Andrea's voice grew excited. "I know Alice would just love this place," she gushed. "She hates the city but stayed for my parents – and me."

The only problem Gloria could see was that even though Alice *said* she hated living in the city, moving to such a small town would be a big change. There were no malls, no coffee shops, only one restaurant...

Andrea answered the question before Gloria could form the words. "She hates the traffic. Hates the noise." She giggled. "I remember one time when she and I tried to grow a garden on the outdoor terrace." She shook her head. "I don't even remember what it was but it never did turn into anything. There wasn't enough light or maybe it was too much smog and it choked the plants."

Gloria could hear the excitement in Andrea's voice. "You mentioned Alice has been around since you were young. Do you have any idea how old she is?" Gloria wondered. Maybe it would be too much for Alice. Change could be hard for people who were older and set in their ways...

Mally wandered over to Andrea's chair and flopped down on top of her feet. Andrea reached down and patted her head. "I'd have to say she's probably about your age. Maybe a little older."

Gloria nodded thoughtfully. The woman might jump at the chance. Gloria knew she would. She shuddered at the thought of living in New York City. She'd never even been there. Never had a desire to go.

The biggest city she'd ever been to was Chicago to see her son, Eddie. Even that was too much. After a few days, Gloria was ready to pack up and head back to her peaceful little town.

"Would you like some tea or lemonade?" Gloria asked.

Andrea shook her head. "I should go back." She ran her fingers through her golden locks. "I fibbed and told them I had to make a quick trip to the post office."

Gloria walked Andrea out to her car. "Have you heard anything from the police on the body or the painting?"

Andrea shook her head. "Nope. Not yet." She grabbed the door handle. "What do you think?"

Gloria wished she'd had a chance to get a better look at the body and the clothing. "The fact that the bones were intact makes me suspect that the body had been planted there. I doubt it was inside your kitchen walls. After all, the construction workers would've noticed it."

Andrea nodded. "That's what I thought." She opened the car door and slid inside. "What about the locked room in the basement?"

"I'm going make a run to the hardware store. Brian might have some ideas on how to pick the lock."

Andrea started her car and rolled the window down.

Gloria leaned in. "Have you ever been in the attic, Andrea?"

Andrea shivered, as if just the thought of the attic gave her the chills. "Nope. I almost went up there once but chickened out."

"Hmm..." The wheels were spinning in Gloria's head.

Andrea slipped on her sunglasses. "I can tell by the look on your face you're dying to check it out."

She put the car in reverse but kept her foot on the brake. "If you *really* want to see it...Why don't you come by the house tomorrow?"

Gloria grinned. "I'll be there in the morning," she promised. Before Andrea could back up, Gloria reached her hand through the open window and touched Andrea's arm. "I know your parents are driving you nuts. Just remember - it's only temporary." She paused. "I like the idea of Alice coming to live with you. You should really think about it."

Andrea promised she'd give it serious thought. Gloria watched as her young friend pulled out of the drive and disappeared down the road. She sent up another small prayer for Andrea and patience as Mally and she wandered inside.

Back inside the house, she picked up her cell phone that was lying on the table. There was a text message. It was from Paul. "I thought you'd never ask! When do you want me? I'm free tonight."

Her heart skipped a beat. It wouldn't give her a lot of time to plan but that was beside the point. Paul was coming over!

With an improved mood, Gloria texted him to come by at 6:00 sharp and that she was making dinner.

She grabbed her purse from the chair, her keys from the rack and headed to the car.   The day was shaping up, after all!

Chapter 6

Gloria's first stop was the hardware store, *Nails and Knobs*. She parked at the end of main street, in front of the store and right next to Brian's SUV. She slid out of Anabelle and headed up the steps.

She opened the front door and stepped inside. A gentle breeze brushed past her. Ceiling fans whirled silently above. Gloria loved how Brian had retained the original charm of the old hardware store. It was like taking a step back in time.

She started down the center aisle and caught a glimpse of him back behind the counter. He grinned when he spotted Gloria. "I've been wondering how long it would take for you to stop by."

Gloria hopped up on the barstool in front of the counter and dropped her purse on top. "You don't say."

Brian nodded. He turned to the small counter behind him. He grabbed a clean cup from the shelf. He poured a cup of coffee and set it in front of Gloria. She took a sip and eyed him over the rim.

Brian wrapped his hands around his own mug and leaned forward. "You're here to pick my brain," he guessed.

"Sort of..."

She reached inside her purse and pulled out her phone. She clicked on the picture of the lock that was hanging on Andrea's basement door. She tapped the screen and made the picture as large as possible before handing the phone to Brian.

"I need to pick this lock or find the key," she told him.

Brian squinted at the screen. He tipped the phone to the side and into the overhead light. "Well, I'll be darned."

He scrolled to the next picture before stopping at the third and final picture. The one she had taken of the back. "Illinois Lock Company," he muttered.

"Is that what it says?" Gloria hadn't been able to read the small print on the back.

He handed the phone back to her. "You're never gonna believe this. Follow me." He signaled her to the back, through the door marked *"Employees Only."*

Gloria hopped down from the stool and followed behind. She had never been in the back of the hardware store. They squeezed in between two rows of cabinets, crammed full of gadgets and gizmos.

He peered at one of the shelves just over Gloria's head. It was loaded with all kinds of locks. He stuck his hand on the shelf and reached around. "It's in here somewhere. I just saw it the other day."

He shoved his hand behind a cardboard box and plucked out a lock. "Aha!" He pulled the lock down and held it out for Gloria to inspect. It was the same exact lock that was on Andrea's basement door! "This it?"

"I do believe it is!" Gloria took the lock from him. "Is there a key?"

"I think so." Brian reached up and felt around the shelf. "Here it is." He pulled his hand out and in it was a silver key. It reminded Gloria of a skeleton key, except this one was thicker and not as long. He handed it to her.

She turned it over. "Do you think it will fit Andrea's lock?"

He shrugged. "It's worth a try."

Gloria looked back at the shelves and the array of locks and stacks of keys. "I wonder if the Johnsons bought their lock here at the store."

The front doorbell tinkled. Someone had come in. Gloria followed Brian back out to the front. He closed the door behind them. "That would make sense."

She nodded. Her detective radar was in high gear. She still had to talk to Doc Decker to see what he remembered about the mysterious people who lived in the mansion.

She added George Ford to her list. George was the original owner of the hardware store.

Gloria glanced at her watch and then reached for her purse. "Thanks for loaning me the key. I'm running by Andrea's tomorrow morning. I'll try it then."

Brian nodded. "Have you met Andrea's parents yet?"

Brian and Andrea had been dating for a few months now. So far, the relationship had Gloria's seal of approval. Brian was turning out to be what Gloria considered excellent husband material: Hardworking, motivated, smart, funny, handsome.

"Yep. I met them this morning. Right after we discovered the body in the dumpster," she added.

Brian respected Gloria's opinion. "I'm curious...." He was about to ask her what she thought, but the customer was standing at the counter, waiting to speak with him. "I'll get back with you later." Gloria nodded and headed for the door.

Next on her list was a stop at the Quik Stop grocery to pick up a couple things for her dinner with Paul. Her heart raced at the thought of spending the evening with him.

With a bounce in her step, Gloria headed down the sidewalk, to the other end of main street and the Quik Stop.

Her cheerful mood abruptly ended when she stepped inside the store. Sally Keane was behind the counter, waiting on a customer. She was grumbling about something. Loudly.

Determined to grab her purchases and make a quick escape before Sally sucked her in with all her moaning and groaning, she grabbed a large bag of shredded cheddar cheese and a jar of olive oil. By the time she reached the checkout counter, the other customer had left.

Gloria was trapped. There was no way to avoid the inevitable conversation. "How are you today, Sally?" She cringed inwardly as she realized that was the wrong thing to ask...

"Well, now that you mention it, I'm having a bad day. I was up all night with gut-wrenching stomach cramps. I'm not sure if the chicken I had at the restaurant last night was bad or if I'm coming down with something." Sally clutched her stomach and moaned. "Oh, there it goes again."

Gloria took a step back. "I'm sorry to hear that." Gloria hoped it was nothing. If not, the woman was either getting sick or had eaten something bad at Dot's place and in that case, everyone who came in the grocery store was going to hear every little detail.

Sally wasn't finished. "On top of that, my car wouldn't start this morning." She put the cheese and olive oil in a small paper bag and took Gloria's money. "I was late for work."

Brian Sellers owned the grocery store, along with the hardware store, and the pharmacy on main street. Gloria was certain Brian would cut Sally some slack if he knew she was having car problems.

Sally shoved the bills in the register and handed Gloria her change. "I need another job. This one just doesn't pay enough or give me enough hours."

"Maybe you should look for something in Green Springs," Gloria suggested. Green Springs was a larger town, not far from Belhaven.

"But that's a long drive, especially in the winter," Sally whined.

Gloria shook her head and tightened her jaw. There was no pleasing this woman! She wondered what on earth Officer Joe saw in her...

As Gloria stepped back out onto the sidewalk, she secretly hoped the woman *would* find another job! One that was far, far away from Belhaven so she wouldn't have to listen to her moaning and groaning any longer!

Gloria hopped in her car and headed back to the farm.

Back in the kitchen, she cleared everything off the table and reached for her apron. She rolled up her sleeves. It was time to fix her chicken cheddar cheese bake. It was a family favorite for as long as Gloria could remember and something she'd never fixed for Paul before.

Gloria switched on the portable radio that sat on the corner shelf behind the kitchen table. Christian music filled the air and Gloria hummed along as she worked.

The afternoon flew by and before Gloria knew it, it was almost time for Paul to arrive. She untied her apron and hung it on the hook near the door. She headed to the bathroom to freshen up.

She made a final comb through her hair when she heard a light tap on the back door. Gloria patted her hair one last time and practically floated to the kitchen. Her heart fluttered at the thought of seeing Paul.

As she rounded the corner of the dining room, she could see his tall frame fill the doorway. She flung the door open and stepped aside.

The smile on his face matched Gloria's own. He leaned down to kiss her lips. When the kiss ended, Gloria leaned her head on his chest, closed her eyes and took a deep breath. She had missed the smell of him. The feel of him. His voice. Tears stung the back of her eyes. She blinked them back quickly as he pulled away.

Paul didn't release her hand. Instead, he pulled her close and kissed her. She started to pull back but he wasn't ready to let her go. He placed his hand behind her head and pulled her even closer, deepening the kiss.

When they finally separated, Gloria's cheeks were flushed and her breathing uneven.

Paul's eyes twinkled. "Now *that* was a kiss," he told her.

Gloria was unnerved. The intensity of the kiss left her breathless.

She jumped to her feet and nearly fell flat on her face in an effort to make a hasty retreat. It was the most intimate kiss they'd shared to date. One that promised so much more. If only...

Paul could tell the kiss had her flustered. Heck, it had flustered him! He decided to change the subject. "The kids are moving out," he announced.

Gloria tugged on the bottom of her silk blouse and spun around to face him. "They are?"

He nodded and grinned. "A week from tomorrow."

Before she could reply, the timer on the stove went off. The cheddar chicken was ready.

Paul hopped out of his chair and headed for the oven. He turned the timer off and grabbed the potholder on top of the stove. He opened the oven door and pulled the baked chicken from the rack. He set the glass dish on the cooktop.

There was another baking dish still in the oven. This one was full of roasted red potatoes. He pulled it out and set it next to the chicken. His mouth watered. "This looks delicious."

Gloria popped a pan of rolls in the hot oven. "We have a few minutes to let these bake. I'll pour a couple lemonades and we can wait out on the porch." She didn't wait for an answer as she grabbed two glasses and filled them with ice.

After she poured the drinks, they stepped outside and settled into the rockers. Mally followed them out. She raced off across the yard when she spied a red squirrel trying to find its way into the bird feeder.

Gloria was beginning to wonder if his kids had any intention of ever moving out. They had settled in quite nicely. Gloria had finally met them a few weeks earlier when Paul invited her over for a cookout. They were nice enough. Very friendly. Very polite. "So what made them change their mind?"

Paul grinned mischievously. "I got a cat."

Gloria was confused. "What does that have to do with motivating them to move?"

Paul sipped his drink. "Tina's allergic to cats." Tina was Paul's daughter-in-law.

Gloria shook her head, but she was smiling. "Paul. That's terrible!" It reminded her of something her mother used to say: *"There's more than one way to skin a cat."*

He rubbed his finger along the rim of the glass. "I admit it was a little underhanded but I was nearing the point of desperation."

He looked up. "Dorito is fitting right in at the farm."

"So how's Tina holding up with the allergies?"

He shook his head. "Not good at all. She's pretty much confined to the bedroom – the only place where the cat is not allowed."

He sighed. "I hated to do it, but I was running out of ideas."

"I told her Dorito was a stray I found down by the station and I didn't have the heart to leave him behind, which was true."

"It was like a gift from heaven. An answer to prayer," he added.

Gloria nodded. Things like that happened to her every once in a while. Where she was in a predicament and it seemed like there was no solution. Suddenly, something would happen and it was like God answering prayer in his own way. Not necessarily a way she would've thought. She firmly believed the saying, *"God works in mysterious ways."*

Paul took the words right out of her head. "God works in mysterious ways."

The timer echoed through the screen door, letting them know the rolls were ready.

Paul held the door as Gloria stepped back inside. He helped set the table while she moved back and forth, arranging the dishes.

She slid into a side chair and he slid into the one next to her. The two of them held hands while Gloria prayed. "Dear Lord, please bless this food. Thank you for letting Paul and I have this evening together. You know how much I've missed him." Paul squeezed her hand.

"Thank you for finding the perfect solution to his problem with his children. Once again, You have taken care of the situation in a way that neither of us would've thought of. We pray for all of our children, for blessings in their lives and for our own. Thank you for Your son, Jesus Christ. In His name we pray. Amen."

"Amen!" Paul lifted his head. He grabbed Gloria's plate, placed a piece of the baked chicken on one side, and then scooped a large spoonful of potatoes on the other side.

At the last minute, Gloria had thrown together a side dish of fresh green beans with bacon bits. He scooped some onto her plate before sliding a piping hot roll in the last remaining spot. He handed the plate to Gloria.

He loaded his plate and set it in front of him. He leaned in. The aroma of baked chicken and cheese filled the air. "This smells heavenly. I haven't had a home-cooked meal since. Well, since you surprised me with that pork chop dinner last month."

After dinner, they wandered out to the porch with a piece of homemade apple pie and cup of coffee. Gloria set her coffee on the stand between the chairs before turning to Paul. "Did you hear about the skeleton we found in Andrea's dumpster?"

Paul nodded. He picked up his fork. "I'm not sure who attracts more bodies – you or Andrea." He lifted a piece of pie to his mouth and took a bite, savoring the tart apple and cinnamon sugar. "This is delicious."

"I threw in a cup of wild blackberries," she told him.

Paul lifted his dessert plate to eye-level and inspected the pie filling. "Yeah, you sure did. The flavor is delicious."

"How's the investigation going?" Gloria wondered.

"The remains are old. Older than Andrea so she's off the hook," he said. "How the remains got in the dumpster is the big mystery. Somebody put that body in there."

Gloria picked up his train of thought. "Hoping that it would just be taken to the landfill and disposed of, never to be seen again."

He nodded. "It would seem that way." He glanced at Gloria. "Do you think there's a connection between the house and the body? Or do you think someone saw the perfect opportunity to get rid of it and they brought it over?"

Gloria remembered Andrea mentioning a while back someone had been inside the house while she was upstairs working in one of the bedrooms. Then there was the locked room in the basement. She absentmindedly reached for the key that Brian had given her, still tucked away in her front pants pocket.

"I have a few people on my list to talk to. People that have lived in Belhaven long enough to remember the Johnsons. They might be able to shed a little light on them. All I remember is that they kept to themselves."

Paul nodded. "I'll let you know what they find out on the remains." The sun had set. All that remained was a bright orange glow.

The two of them wandered back in the house. Gloria rinsed the dishes while Paul loaded them in the dishwasher. He glanced up at the clock. "I should get going. I have to work early tomorrow."

Gloria was a bit disappointed he had to leave so soon. She followed him to his car and watched as he unlocked the doors. Instead of opening the door, he swung around, grabbed her by the elbow and pulled her close. She wrapped her arms around his neck and stood up on her tiptoes as he lowered his head to kiss her. After a long, lingering kiss, he reluctantly released his hold.

She stuck the palms of her hands on his chest. The garage light picked up the colors in the ring and it sparkled brightly. "Thanks again for the beautiful ring. I just love it," she gushed.

"It was a toss-up. Either the ring or flowers," he teased.

He climbed into his car and rolled down the window before starting the engine. "I'm off next weekend and the kids should be out by then. It's my turn to make dinner."

"Is that an invitation?" she flirted.

"Don't expect too much," he warned. "You know the only thing I'm capable of is grilling."

"Sounds perfect." She leaned her head in the window and kissed him on the lips before easing back out. "It's a date."

Gloria watched as Paul backed out of the driveway and pulled out onto the road. A small smile played across her lips. She nearly floated down the sidewalk and into the house. Once again, all was right in Gloria's world!

Chapter 7

Gloria's eyes flew open and immediately zeroed in on the nightstand next to her bed and the jewelry box where she had carefully placed her new ring the night before. She leaned over and grabbed the box. She lifted the ring from the inside and slipped it on her finger. She admired it for several long moments before sliding into her slippers and shuffling out to the kitchen.

It had been a restless night, full of tossing and turning. Her mind had darted back and forth between her evening with Paul the night before and wondering how on earth the skeleton got inside the dumpster. During the long hours she was awake, she managed to make a long mental to-do list. The first thing on her list was a visit to Doc Decker.

Mally was waiting for Gloria on the other side of the bedroom door and the two of them wandered out into the kitchen. Gloria scrambled two eggs and made some toast with an extra slice for Mally. She lathered the top with thick layer of peanut butter and cut it into bite size pieces before putting it on a paper plate and setting it on the floor.

Puddles was next. Gloria scooped a small pile of scrambled eggs onto a second paper plate and set it on the floor. Puddles nibbled the edge of Gloria's hand to show his appreciation before he started to eat his treat.

The three of them enjoyed their morning breakfast in silence. Gloria's head was spinning with scenarios on how the body made it into the dumpster.

She loaded the last bit of egg onto her toast and folded it in half. In two bites, the food was gone and Gloria was ready to start her day.

She took a quick shower then pulled on a pair of pink capris and white cotton blouse. She slid her feet into a pair of her favorite sandals, grabbed her keys and hopped in the car. She rolled down main street and passed by Dot's on her way through town. The breakfast crowd was in full swing and the place packed.

Doc Decker and his wife, Martha, lived in a rambling, two-story Victorian only a block from the old elementary school. They had lived in the house for as long as Gloria could remember. It was here the couple had raised their five children and then stayed on in Belhaven, even after they closed the old drug store and retired.

Gloria would drive down their street every so often, just to scope out Martha's landscaping. The woman had a green thumb and Gloria was always a bit envious of the lush lawn and beautiful flowers and plants.

She thought about calling ahead but knew that they, like many of the other retired residents of Belhaven, were most likely at home puttering around the house.

Gloria pulled Anabelle in past the white picket fence and parked behind a tan minivan. She pulled her purse off the seat and slid out of the car.

She glanced up at the beautiful leaded glass window on the second floor before turning her attention to the blooming Dahlias planted on both sides of the front walk as she made her way to the front porch.

She pressed the doorbell and waited. Gloria could hear a faint shuffling from within. Out of the corner of her eye, she caught a glimpse of the lace curtains as they moved, right before the door opened.

Martha Decker's tiny frame appeared on the other side of the screen. "Hello Gloria. What a pleasant surprise!" She pushed the wooden frame door wide and shuffled to the side. "C'mon in." Gloria crossed over the threshold and into the crowded living room.

Several large pieces of furniture surrounded the brick fireplace on the far wall. A row of tall curio cabinets lined the wall opposite the fireplace. On the other side were two recliners, separated by a small farmhouse table.

Martha talked as she walked. "Would you like a cup of coffee?" She didn't wait for a reply. Instead, she continued down the wide hall towards the back of the house.

Gloria followed behind. When she reached the kitchen, she found Doc Decker sitting at the kitchen table, drinking a cup of coffee and reading the morning paper. He snapped the paper in his hands. His eyes shot up as he peered at her over the top of his reading glasses. "If it isn't Gloria Rutherford." He set the paper down and maneuvered around in his chair. "Heard they found a body in the dumpster out at the old Johnson mansion."

His head, bald except for a wisp or two of hair, tipped to the side as he talked.

Gloria nodded. "That's why I'm here. I was hoping you'd be able to tell me what you can remember about the last family of Johnsons that lived in the old place.

Doc Decker nodded. He lifted his coffee cup and shoved the paper underneath before setting the cup back down. He stuck his elbow on the table and rubbed his hand across his brow. "Been a long time. I'm not sure how much I remember about them."

Martha pulled out the chair opposite Doc and set a cup of coffee on the table in front of it. "Here. Have a seat."

"Thank you." Gloria slid into the chair and reached for the coffee. "Just tell me whatever comes to mind."

Doc pulled his glasses off and set them on the newspaper. "Well, Abe and Barbara moved into that old place after Abe's parents died. They took over the mill and ran it for many years until Abe's accident."

Gloria wrapped her hands around the porcelain mug. "Are you saying that Abe Johnson *owned* the mill?" That was the first she'd ever heard of the Johnsons owning the mill. Eleanor Whittaker had said that he worked there. Not owned it.

Doc nodded. "Yep. Had a successful business there until he sold it." He leaned forward. "Your mother. She worked there for a short time in the office."

Gloria's forehead crinkled. Her mother never mentioned that she'd worked at the mill...

"Course, it wasn't very long at all." He paused. "It's probably not my place to say, but there was some sort of fracas that happened over there and your father made her quit."

Gloria raised her eyebrows. Never in her life had she heard this story. "What about some of the other locals? Did anyone else work there?"

"Well, there was Matt Whittaker."

Gloria nodded. Eleanor had already told her that.

He went on. "George Ford worked there for a while, too. Before he bought the hardware store."

Doc Decker scratched his head. "That's about it. Other than Abe's brother, Hank."

Gloria arched her brow. "Abe had a brother?"

Martha reached under the table and squeezed her husband's leg. He gave her a quick look and continued. "Stepbrother. He was a troublemaker. Always getting into fights with town folk, right up until the day he disappeared."

Gloria's eyes widened. "He disappeared?"

Doc nodded. "Abe told everyone he went back home to Pennsylvania. Not that anyone minded. Good riddance to the rascal. That's what we all thought." Doc picked up his coffee cup and took a sip. "Ain't much else to remember."

"You've been very helpful." Gloria downed the last bit of coffee and got to her feet. She turned to Martha and smiled. "Thanks for the coffee."

Martha and Doc walked Gloria to the front door. "If I think of anything else, I'll give you a call," Doc promised.

Gloria pulled her keys from her purse and stepped onto the porch. "I'd appreciate that, Doc."

The two of them stood at the door and watched as Gloria climbed into her car and backed out of the drive.

Gloria took the back way home, passing by the old elementary school. Her mind was spinning. Her mother had worked at the old mill? Abe had a stepbrother who "disappeared?" Was Abe's brother the body they found in the dumpster? If it was, how did it get there?

Gloria's next stop was Andrea's place. She was anxious to see if the key she'd borrowed from Brian would fit in that lock!

Gloria let out a sigh of relief as she pulled in the drive. The limo was gone, which meant Andrea's parents weren't around. Her parents made her a bit uncomfortable, especially her father. She got the distinct impression that he did not like Gloria very much.

Gloria trotted to the front door and smiled as she reached for the lion's head. She gave the iron ring two sharp raps and waited.

Seconds later, Andrea swung the door open and stepped aside. Brutus wiggled past Andrea. Gloria leaned down and patted his head. "Good morning, Brutus." He wagged his tail then licked her hand before sticking his nose on her pant leg. "You smell Mally, don't you?"

Andrea wrinkled her nose. "I guess this means you're serious about checking out the locked room in the basement."

Gloria pulled the key from her front pocket and held it up for Andrea to see. "Aren't you the least bit curious to find out what might be inside?"

Andrea shuddered. "What if there are more bodies?"

Gloria shifted her weight. She hadn't considered that. It would present a bit of a problem but Gloria didn't think that was what was inside. Of course, she could be wrong...

Gloria followed Andrea down the basement steps and over to the small locked door. Her heart pounded as she stuck the key in the lock. It fit perfectly! The only problem was, it wouldn't turn. Her heart sank. "It fits but it won't unlock it." She pulled the useless key from the lock and turned it over in her hand.

Andrea almost seemed relieved. She stood up and brushed the dirt from her pants. "Well, I guess it'll just have to stay a mystery," she concluded.

The girls headed up the stairs and into the hall.

Gloria looked towards the stairs leading up to the second floor. "What about the attic?"

Andrea rubbed the sides of her arms and studied her friend's expression. "I was hoping you'd forget," she admitted.

It was wishful thinking on Andrea's part. She could tell from the look on Gloria's face that she had every intention of finding out what was in that attic!

Andrea's shoulder drooped. "Okay. Let's go." She looked down at Brutus. "You're going with us for protection."

Gloria chuckled. "Protect us from what? Ghosts?" The smile left her face when she saw the look Andrea gave her. It was exactly what Andrea feared. That some sort of spirit dwelt in her attic.

Andrea reluctantly started up the steps with Gloria close behind.

At the center landing, she turned right and headed toward the guest wing. "The only way into the attic is through the room my parents are staying in," Andrea explained.

She opened the door at the end of the long hall and stepped inside. Gloria followed her to the closet. Andrea opened the closet door and flipped on the light. The closet was long and narrow.

Andrea made her way to the back and pushed a row of clothing to the side to reveal another door. "This is it," she announced. She squeezed past Gloria until she was standing behind her. "You go first."

Gloria stared at the door. Now that she was here, she wasn't 100% convinced she wanted to find out what was in the attic. She took a deep breath and swallowed hard before grabbing the knob. It was now or never.

Gloria started to twist the knob and then stopped. "Do you think we'll need a flashlight?"

"Maybe." Andrea didn't wait for a reply as she turned on her heel and headed out of the closet. She ran down to the kitchen and grabbed a couple flashlights from under the kitchen sink.

She headed back up the steps and into the closet where Gloria was still waiting, her hand still gripping the knob.

She stuck a flashlight in Gloria's outstretched hand. "You have to admit, this is freaking you out," Andrea said breathlessly.

Gloria nodded. Yes. It was more than a little spooky. After all, who knew how many years it had been since anyone had stepped foot inside the attic.

"I have something to tell you but I'll wait 'til later," Andrea blurted out.

Gloria sucked in a breath. She turned the knob and the door creaked open. A sliver of light shined in through a small, round window on the far wall. The room was long and narrow.

Gloria switched the flashlight on and beamed the bright light around the room. The floor covering was some sort of wooden floorboard. Thick wooden rafters covered both sides of the a-frame shape.

Gloria stepped inside. The floorboard groaned under her weight, as if in protest. Andrea clutched the bottom of Gloria's blouse and followed her into the room.

Gloria ran the light along the rafters in search of a non-existent light bulb.

Lined along the right hand wall were several boxes. Except for those few boxes, the room was empty.

Andrea shivered. Her eyes wandered up as she studied the ceiling. They traveled along the center beam before focusing on the round window on the far wall. "This place is giving me the heebie-jeebies."

Brutus wandered into the attic and perched next to Andrea's feet. He let out a low growl and his ears tipped back.

Andrea patted the top of his head. "He doesn't like this place, either."

Gloria wasn't too keen on it herself. It almost felt as if someone was watching them, which was impossible. There was no one else in the attic, or even in the house for that matter. "Let's grab the boxes and get out of here!"

"Right!" Andrea stepped over to the small stack of boxes and picked up two of them. Gloria grabbed the other two boxes.

A tingle of fear spread down Gloria's spine and the hair on the back of her neck stood up. The sensation of someone watching them grew stronger.

Brutus glared at the far corner and let out a second low growl.

The girls darted from the room. Brutus was close behind.

Back in the closet, Andrea grabbed the door handle and slammed the door shut. For good measure, she pushed on it.

They carried the boxes out of the closet and through the bedroom. "My parents are leaving in a couple days." Andrea shifted the boxes she was carrying.

"I was wondering how much longer they would be here," Gloria replied. "Where are they today?"

Andrea rolled her eyes. "They told me they were heading into Green Springs to find decent coffee. I guess mine's not good enough."

When they got to the hall, Andrea pulled the bedroom door closed behind her. "Pretty soon that'll be Alice's room."

That made Gloria pause. "Alice is coming?"

Andrea raised her eyebrows. "Oh! With everything going on, I forgot to tell you. Yeah! Alice is coming to live with me!"

The girls headed down the stairs and made their way into the kitchen. Andrea set the small boxes on the kitchen bar top. "C'mon. I want to show you something."

Gloria followed her young friend out the back door and into the yard. The girls stopped a short distance from the house and Andrea pointed up. "See? There's the attic window."

Gloria followed her gaze and nodded. "Yeah."

She shaded her eyes from the bright sun and looked at Gloria. "Sometimes I could swear I see a face staring out at me or feel eyes following me."

A shiver ran down Gloria's spine. It was the same feeling that Gloria felt when they were inside the attic. "But there's no one there."

Andrea crossed her arms. "I'm never going back in the attic. I think I'll have Brian nail the door shut. Just in case," she added.

Gloria followed Andrea back into the kitchen. Andrea grabbed a couple of bottled waters from the fridge before the women settled in at the kitchen bar.

Andrea pulled the first box from the stack and opened it. The box contained some old dishes wrapped in newspaper. She unwrapped each piece and lined them up on the edge of the counter. "These are cool. I should put them in my china cabinet."

Andrea had picked up a beautiful antique china cabinet at one of the thrift stores in Green Springs. She had managed to match the color and grain of wood to her antique dining room table. The large pieces of furniture filled the room. It was comfortable. Cozy.

Andrea reached for the second box. "Did I tell you I'm adding a sunroom on the other side of the living room?"

Gloria shook her head. That was the first she'd heard of a sunroom. Although it would be the perfect spot for one. It faced the east and the morning sun would brighten it right up. Plus, Andrea had planted a large, flowering garden on that side of the house. A sunroom overlooking her garden would be perfect.

"No, but I think that's a great idea," she said. "What with the long winters, it would really warm the place up."

"Exactly," Andrea said. She opened the second box. It was full of the same sort of dishes.

The third box was a surprise. In it were several small paintings. She pulled the first one from the pile and laid it on the counter between them.

Gloria slipped on her glasses and leaned in. "Will you look at that," she murmured under her breath. The painting reminded her of the one they had found on the piece of paneling. Except instead of a portrait of a young woman, this one was of a large, cream-colored vase with an array of bright flowers bursting out.

Andrea pushed the first painting to the side and pulled a second one from the stack. This one was of a flower garden, eerily similar to the one Andrea had created in the backyard.

There were five paintings in all. In addition to the vase and the rose garden, there was one of a man in a top hat, and another of a horse drawn carriage. The horse was pulling the carriage down a narrow cobblestone street. Small brick shops lined both sides of the street.

When Andrea pulled the last small painting from the box, they both gasped. Gloria covered her mouth with her hand. It was a painting of Andrea's house. What it must have looked like when it was new. Two gas lanterns adorned each side of the massive front door.

Gloria leaned in. She pointed at the door. "Is that what I think it is?"

Andrea sucked in a breath. "It's an old door knocker. An old door knocker with a lion's head!"

In front of the porch was another horse-drawn carriage. A woman wearing a long, flowing ballroom gown had one foot on the top step of the carriage. A gray-haired man with a pencil-thin moustache, wearing a long, ornate jacket and a pair of breeches was holding her hand, helping her out. It reminded Gloria of something out of Cinderella but instead of a castle, they were in front of Andrea's house.

Andrea rubbed the tip of her finger over the surface. "This is the coolest picture I've ever seen."

Gloria had to agree. It was an amazing painting. She glanced at the paintings carefully laid out on the counter top. They were all magnificent.

"I'm going to frame this and hang it in the living room," she decided. Andrea placed the paintings back in the box. She put the one of the house on top of the stack.

There was one box left. She pulled it forward and lifted the lid. The box was full of faded black and white photos. They carefully sifted through the stack as they studied them one-by-one. "These must belong to the Johnson family. I should send them to the family."

Gloria nodded, certain the family would appreciate the gesture. They were almost to the bottom of the pile when one caught Gloria's eye. "Wait! Let me see that."

Andrea slid the picture across the granite counter. Gloria picked it up and pulled it close to her face. It was the old grain mill in town! Standing in front of the mill were several people.

In small, handwritten letters were the names of the people in the picture. "George Ford, Matthew Whittaker, Hank Johnson, Abe Johnson," she whispered. At the end of the row was a young woman. She was standing next to Abe Johnson, who towered over her.

Gloria's heart sank. There was no name indicating who the woman was. She tilted the picture to get a better view in the light. *Was that her mother?* she wondered. It was hard to tell. The image was grainy. It was possible. Who else could it be? Unless it was Abe's wife, Barbara. But the woman was young. A lot younger than Abe. Had Abe Johnson's wife been decades younger?

She glanced at Andrea. "Do you mind if I borrow this picture?"

Andrea shrugged. "No. Not at all." She looked up at her friend. "You think this is a clue?"

Gloria nodded. She narrowed her eyes and studied the people one more time. None of the men looked like they were capable of killing Hank Johnson. Then again, maybe he hadn't been murdered. Maybe he had gone back to Pennsylvania, just as Abe had told everyone. Still, the skeleton in the dumpster was decades old.

Gloria couldn't wait to find out what the autopsy revealed. That would tell them a great deal about the body.

In the distance, she heard a car door slam. Andrea's parents and Pierce were back.

Gloria hopped down off the barstool. "I really should go," she said.

"You don't have to leave." Andrea's eye pleaded. "Won't you please stay? Help me entertain them?"

Gloria gave Andrea's arm a reassuring squeeze. "You can do this! Remember, they won't be here much longer."

She lifted her purse and the photo from the counter. "Isn't Brian coming by?"

Andrea glanced at the clock. "He'll be here at six. We're grilling steaks."

"See? Everything will be just fine," Gloria told her. Andrea led her to the front door. They passed Andrea's parents on their way in. Her mother had taken the surgical mask off but was still wearing the gloves.

Pierce gave her a warm smile. Andrea's father gave her a cold stare.

Gloria said a small prayer for Brian. Hopefully, Andrea's father would take more of a liking to poor Brian.

She climbed in the car and started the engine. It was time to pay a visit to George Ford.

Chapter 8

George and his wife, Maxine, had lived in the back of the Belhaven hardware store for decades. When they sold the place to Brian, they moved into a quaint, blue bungalow on the hill just outside of town. At the time they bought it, it was a real fixer-upper, but George was handy and he had managed to turn the place into a beautiful, cozy home. It was the perfect size for just the two of them.

Maxine's health was declining. She'd had a stroke a year or so ago and now George was responsible for her day-to-day care.

The Garden Girls had added them to their list a while back and faithfully visited them every Sunday, bringing fresh fruits and vegetables from their gardens. When Gloria remembered or had time, she'd bake an extra loaf of bread or batch of cookies and take them with her.

George always appreciated a homemade treat. Gloria was sure he did the best he could, but Maxine had been the chief cook and bottle washer for most of their marriage.

Maxine was in a wheelchair these days and George had purchased a special van to lift the wheelchair in and out of the van when they had to leave the house.

The two of them seemed like the perfect couple. They had raised their only son, John, in the back of the hardware store. John, like many of the others that had grown up in the area, had gone off to college and then moved away. Gloria remembered Maxine telling her that he lived out in California now.

Gloria parked her car next to their van and made her way up the wheelchair ramp to the front door. She raised her hand to knock when George quietly opened the door. "Hello Gloria." He frowned. "Do I have my days mixed up?"

Gloria chuckled. "No, George. It's not Sunday."

He waved his hand. "Naw! I was teasing! I talked to Doc earlier today. He said you were poking around, trying to find out what you could about Abe Johnson."

Gloria knew what he *really* meant was "snoop" but he was too nice to say it.

"Come on in!" He motioned her inside.

Gloria followed him through the small breezeway and into the tidy living room. Maxine was in a recliner, watching TV. She smiled brightly. "Oh! Hi Gloria!"

Gloria walked over to the recliner. She leaned down and gave Maxine a gentle hug. "Don't you look sunny today," she complimented.

"I feel pretty darned chipper," Maxine replied. She eyed her husband. "Course that's because George takes such good care of me."

A look passed between the two and Gloria felt a twinge of envy. If James had still been alive, he would've done the same thing. Taken care of Gloria until he breathed his last. Unexpected tears burned the back of her eyes.

She shook off the moment and focused on her friend.

Maxine waved to the couch. "Have a seat."

Gloria sat on the edge of the sofa and smoothed the brown cloth that covered the armrest.

Maxine's sharp eye noticed Gloria's ring. "What a beautiful ring," she exclaimed.

Gloria glanced down. She'd almost forgotten about it. Almost.

She lifted her arm and flashed her ring finger in Maxine's direction. "Thanks. Paul gave it to me last night."

Maxine adjusted the afghan around her legs. "So that means you're getting married?"

Gloria's cheeks warmed. "Uh, n-not yet," she stuttered.

Maxine could see she'd put Gloria on the spot. She quickly changed the subject. "I heard they found a skeleton out in the dumpster at the old Johnson mansion."

Gloria nodded. "Yeah. I'm trying to find out more about the Johnsons. You know, a little bit of history and what-not."

George settled into the recliner next to his wife's. "I worked there at the old mill for a few years. Back before I bought the hardware store."

Gloria nodded. She wasn't ready to tell anyone about the photo. The one she and Andrea had found in the attic earlier. "I heard Abe Johnson had a stepbrother, Hank, and that he worked at the mill for a few months."

George's expression grew grim. "He was nothin' but trouble."

"That's what Doc told me. That he got into fights and such and then one day he disappeared."

George reached for a glass of water that was on the stand next to him. He took a big gulp. Gloria noticed his knuckles turned white as he clenched the glass in a tight grip. Apparently, he wasn't too fond of Hank, either.

"Caught him trying to steal from me," he admitted.

"Now, George." Maxine shook her head.

George gave his wife a dark look. "True. I couldn't outright prove it but I'd bet my life on it."

He went on. "Course, we always heard that he moved back to Pennsylvania. That Abe kicked him out of the house after they got into an argument."

Gloria shifted in her seat. She had to wonder if there was a single person in the whole town that liked the guy. Even so, could he have done something so horrible someone killed him?

Maxine gasped and clutched at her chest. She began to cough violently. George jumped up from his chair and wrapped an arm around her shoulders. He eased his wife upright. "Take slow breaths. Relax."

Gloria stood up. "I should go. I hope I didn't upset her," she fretted.

George looked up. "No. She's okay."

Gloria let herself out of the house and got into her car. It was obvious the subject of Hank Johnson brought back bad memories, even after all these years.

She made a last minute decision to swing by Lucy's place on her way home. Gloria was glad to see only Lucy's jeep parked in the driveway and not her boyfriend, Bill's. It wasn't that she didn't like Bill. It was just that the girls couldn't really talk when he was around.

She climbed out of the car and started down the sidewalk.

KABOOM!

A loud noise, something akin to a mini-explosion, filled the air. The ground shook under Gloria's feet.

Gloria darted off the sidewalk in the direction of the noise. There, on the far side of the garden, was Lucy.

Lucy, decked out in camo gear and holding a handgun, was marching towards a tall stack of crates not far from an outbuilding.

She watched as Lucy slid a set of earmuffs from her ears and let them dangle around her neck. She leaned forward and muttered loudly as she studied an object perched on top of the crate.

"What on earth are you doing?" Gloria exclaimed.

Lucy spun around, the gun still in her hand.

Gloria raised her hands above her head. "Don't shoot!" she shouted.

Lucy grinned and set the gun on the ground before she wandered over to where Gloria was standing. "You scared me," she said.

"*I* scared *you*?" Gloria sputtered. "I'm not the one with the gun!" she pointed out.

Lucy ignored the comment. "C'mere. You gotta check this out." She didn't wait for Gloria to reply as she turned on her heel and headed to the stack of crates.

Lucy pointed at the top of the crate. "I've been practicing my shot."

On top of the stack of crates, strategically resting in the center, was a watermelon. In the center of the melon was a large, gaping hole.

Inside the hole was a round, yellow disc. Gloria pointed at the disc. "What in heaven's name is that?"

Lucy stuck her hands on her hips. "It's an exploding target. You know, KABOOM!"

Gloria reached over and stuck her hand on Lucy's forehead. "I need to get you to the hospital. You're delusional," she decided.

Lucy swatted Gloria's hand away. "Naw! It's just a small one. You know, just big enough to blow up small things like watermelons. Or potatoes," she added.

"Whatever possessed you to set off explosives?" Gloria asked. She held up her hands. "No! Wait! Let me guess...this was *Bill's* idea."

Lucy nodded. "Yeah! But it's fun. It's like target practice on steroids," she explained.

Gloria had heard it all now. She shook her head. "Isn't it illegal to buy explosives?"

Lucy wrinkled her nose. "We don't *buy* these. We make 'em," she informed Gloria.

Gloria leaned in to study the yellow disc. "You built that?" She shook her head. "No! I don't want to know."

"I'll be right back." Lucy picked up the gun and headed to the garage to put it away. She returned a few minutes later. "So what brings you by?"

"My head is spinning over this skeleton in the dumpster," she admitted. She trailed behind Lucy as they headed up the steps and indoors.

Lucy washed her hands at the sink before she filled a teakettle with tap water. She set the kettle on the stove and turned the burner on.

She leaned against the counter and faced her friend. "I've heard bits and pieces but only that the body is old, which gets Andrea off the hook for a change. Rumor has it that the body might belong to Abe Johnson's stepbrother, Hank, who mysteriously disappeared."

Gloria nodded. The teakettle started to whistle. Lucy grabbed two teacups from the cupboard, dropped a tea bag inside each cup and then filled them with hot water.

She carried them to the table before reaching into the small pantry next to the fridge. Lucy pulled out a plastic container filled with cookies.

Gloria eyed the cookies with interest and reached for the container. "What kind are these?"

"Variety pack." Lucy them on the table.

Gloria's ring caught the kitchen light.

"Oh my gosh!" Lucy grabbed Gloria's hand. "Did you get a new ring?"

Gloria blushed. "Yeah, Paul gave it to me last night."

"Does this mean wedding bells will be chiming in the near future?"

"He didn't ask me to marry him," Gloria said.

Lucy opened the container and pulled out a peanut butter cookie. She took a big bite then set it on the napkin in front of her.

Gloria grabbed an oatmeal raisin cookie and nibbled on the edge. "His kids are finally moving out."

"Well, thank the Lord," Lucy exclaimed. She'd listened to Gloria grumble about it for weeks now. "How'd he managed that?"

Lucy smiled as Gloria told her the story about the cat and how Tina, his daughter-in-law, was allergic to them. "That was a good idea."

Lucy sipped her hot tea and reached for a second cookie. This time, she went for the chocolate chip. "So tell me what you know about the body."

"Not much." Gloria remembered the photo. "I'll be right back."

She walked out to the car, grabbed the picture off the passenger seat and headed back inside. By now, Lucy was on cookie number three.

Gloria shook her head. "If I ate cookies that fast, I'd have a stomach ache."

Lucy nodded. "It takes practice. Years of practice. Kind of like getting ready for a marathon. Cookie-eating is like endurance-building."

Gloria glanced down at her napkin. She was still working on her oatmeal raisin cookie. She put the photo on the table and slid it towards her friend.

Lucy grabbed her reading glasses from a stack of papers nearby and slipped them on. She picked the photo up and studied it. "Who's the woman on the end?"

"My mother," Gloria answered. "Maybe," she added.

Lucy's head shot up. "Your mother? She worked at the mill?"

"That's what Doc Decker told me. He said she didn't work there very long. Something happened and my dad made her quit."

Lucy devoured two more cookies as Gloria told her the story of Abe owning the mill. She went on to explain how his stepbrother had come to work for him for a short time until he mysteriously disappeared.

She also told her how everyone she'd talked to disliked the man.

"So you're thinking the remains in the dumpster belong to this Hank Johnson," Lucy said. She glanced out the window. "Bill's here."

Gloria stood. "What are you two up to today? Blowing more stuff up?"

"We're going to look at quads," she said.

Gloria reached for her purse. "You mean those four-wheel thingys?"

Lucy nodded. "Yeah, they'd be pretty fun to take out back in the fields and ride around. You know, look for deer and stuff."

Gloria could picture Lucy, a rifle slung over her shoulder, as she rode around the fields in search of helpless prey. She shook her head. "How about a lunch date in Grand Rapids? We can go shopping."

Lucy walked her to her car as Bill got out of his truck.

Gloria smiled and nodded but didn't stop to talk.

"I'd like that," Lucy told her as Gloria slipped in the driver's seat.

Gloria started her car and headed to the road. In her rearview mirror, she watched as Bill slung his arm around Lucy's shoulders and they walked inside.

Lucy really seemed to like Bill. Gloria only wished he'd do a little more of what Lucy was interested in. Of course, she seemed pretty excited about blowing stuff up, which concerned Gloria a bit.

Chapter 9

Back at the farm, Gloria rambled around the yard. She wandered over to the garden to water it then stepped back inside. She looked around her kitchen, still feeling as if she needed something to do.

Maybe it was time for a long overdue visit from her grandsons, Tyler and Ryan.

Gloria picked up the phone and dialed her daughter's number. Jill picked up on the first ring. "Hi Mom."

"Hello Jill. How are you?"

Jill let out a long, aggravated sigh. "I'll be glad when school starts. The boys are driving me nuts!" she admitted.

Gloria grinned. Yes, her grandsons could be a handful. What they needed was some fresh, country air! Somewhere to run around and release some of that pent up energy! "That's why

I'm calling. To ask if they could come spend the night."

"Seriously? They would love it. I would love it," Jill told her.

"How about tomorrow night? I can catch up on some things here around the house and then I'll have plenty of time to spend with them tomorrow."

Before she hung up, Jill told her they'd see her around noon the next day and she'd bring the boys overnight bags.

Gloria hung up the phone, pleased that she would not only be able to spend time with her precious grandsons, but that her daughter could have a much-needed break.

Gloria spent the rest of the afternoon cleaning the house, mopping floors, and doing some laundry. As she worked, her mind wandered to the paintings. She thought about the body and

Hank Johnson. Her gut told her the remains in the dumpster belonged to him.

What if Abe was the killer? What if they had gotten into an argument and Abe had hid his body? But Abe was long gone. That meant someone else knew about Hank's body. Someone that lived in the small, quiet town of Belhaven.

Gloria finally finished all her housework and plopped down in the kitchen chair. She wasn't in the mood to cook. She wasn't in the mood for Dot's, either. She thought about her sister, Liz, whom she hadn't seen her in quite some time. She picked her cell phone off the table and dialed Liz's number.

The phone rang and rang. Gloria was almost ready to hang up when a breathless Liz answered. "Hello?"

"Hey Liz. Everything okay? You sound like you just ran around the block," Gloria told her.

"I wish that was all it was," Liz moaned. "Frances is driving me crazy." Frances was Liz's closest friend. They both lived in Dreamwood Retirement Community in nearby Green Springs.

Jill had been trying to talk her mother into moving there for a couple years now. Something that Gloria was bound and determined *not* to do.

There was way too much drama at that place. Not only that, her sister, Liz, was almost always right in the thick of it!

"What's wrong with Frances?" Hard telling with Frances. She and Liz were a lot alike. Maybe that was why they were so close. From one drama queen to another...

"Milt is missing," Liz told her.

Milt was Frances's love interest. Frances had been chasing poor Milt for years now. He was one of only a handful of eligible bachelors that lived in Dreamwood. He had at least a dozen women at any given time waiting on his beck and call. "Maybe he ran off with one of his girlfriends."

"Yeah. We should be so lucky," Liz muttered. She changed the subject. "So what's new with you?"

Gloria scratched a small speck off the kitchen counter with her fingernail. She wiped it into the sink. "I was trying to decide what to do for dinner and thought of you. Are you free?"

That seemed to cheer Liz up. "Yeah! I need something to take my mind off Milt," she said wryly.

Before she hung up, Gloria agreed to meet Liz at her apartment and then they would run over to the community cafeteria for dinner. Gloria made a quick trip to the bathroom to freshen up before she grabbed her purse and car keys.

Mally pulled herself from her doggy bed. She wagged her tail at Gloria, who paused for a fraction of a second. The residents at

Dreamwood loved Mally and were always so excited when Gloria brought her by. "Okay, girl. You can come too!" Mally darted to the door, a one-eyed teddy bear firmly clenched in her jaw.

Mally climbed in the passenger side, riding shotgun, which was her normal place in the car if Gloria didn't have someone else tagging along.

The evening air was warm. Gloria rolled down the front windows to let the fresh air in. Mally hung her head out the passenger door for most of the ride.

Gloria grinned when she noticed her tongue hanging out of her mouth, a smile on her face.

She pulled the car into a visitor parking spot, directly across from Liz's shiny new four-door sedan. The two of them climbed out of the car and headed to the slider out front.

Liz was waiting for them. She flung the door open before she reached down and patted Mally's head. "Look who we have here – my favorite super dog!"

She rubbed Mally's ears. "I have something for you," she told her. Ever since Mally had saved the girls' lives up in the mountains, Mally held a special place in Liz's heart.

She trotted off to the kitchen and came back moments later with a surprise, which Mally gratefully accepted. She licked Liz's hand in a show of appreciation before grabbing the doggie treat in her mouth and wandering over to the corner to devour the tasty morsel.

Gloria watched the exchange. "So what's this about Milt being missing?"

Liz looked up. "He disappeared a couple days ago. No one has seen hide nor hair of him. Frances is freaking out."

The three of them stepped onto the sidewalk. Liz locked the door behind them.

It was a short walk to Dreamwood's main restaurant, "Dreamwood Eats." There was one other restaurant in the complex, "Fifth Plate." It was more of an upscale restaurant for special occasions. The only other place to grab a bite to eat was the snack shack inside the clubhouse, near the golf course.

Gloria had to admit Dreamwood had a ton of activities for residents. It just wasn't her thing. At least not yet. Perhaps it was something else that stopped her from seriously considering a move. Gloria thought in the back of her mind if she moved to a place like Dreamwood, she'd be surrendering some of her independence.

Liz seemed to love it. She held the door and waited as Gloria and Mally stepped inside. The place was busy and it was only 5:00 in the afternoon.

Gloria glanced at the signboard on the way to the back. "Today's special is liver and onions."

She wrinkled her nose. She wasn't too picky of an eater but she hated liver and onions.

Liz grinned, fully aware of Gloria's aversion to the special. "I'm sure you can find something else to eat."

They made their way over to the end of the line. Gloria grabbed a tray then handed one to Liz. The smell of fresh baked bread filled the air. Her stomach grumbled as she set the tray on the metal runner.

Gloria started with a small side salad and moved onto the hot items. She set two pieces of meatloaf off to the side, grabbed a bowl of mashed potatoes and brown gravy before sliding forward.

It was then she spied the fried chicken. Her mouth watered. She glanced down at her plate. There was plenty of room for a piece of chicken. She set it on her plate and added a mound of corn to the small space she had left.

"The raspberry tea is really good," Liz told her.

Raspberry tea sounded perfect. Gloria grabbed a plastic cup, filled it half full of ice and then topped it off with the tea.

She and Mally waited for Liz at the end of the line. "Where do you want to sit?" She glanced around the room. A few of the faces looked familiar but the names... Gloria had a hard time remembering names. She tried word association. Sometimes that worked but there were times it backfired on her. Like the time she called Harry Washenter, one of the residents – Henry Kissinger. It was an honest mistake but Liz still teased her about it.

Liz pointed with one finger, her hand still gripping the heavy tray. "Over there. I see a couple open chairs next to Frances."

Gloria and Mally followed Liz to the empty seats. Gloria set her tray on the table and settled in. Thankfully, she had remembered to grab a paper plate from the food line. She lifted a slice of meatloaf from her own plate and chopped it into small pieces.

She put the pieces on the paper plate and set it on the floor beside her. Mally licked her hand in appreciation before turning to the tasty morsels.

Gloria turned to Frances. "Heard anything from Milt?"

Liz narrowed her eyes and shook her head - but it was too late.

France lifted her head. Her eyes filled with tears. "Not a peep," she answered sorrowfully.

Gloria quickly changed the subject. She pointed to the front doors. "I noticed they're having a dance here tomorrow night," she said.

Unfortunately, that didn't seem to help matters as a tear trickled down poor Frances's face. "Milt was going to take me."

Liz scowled at Gloria and turned to her friend. "Did you hear about the body they found out in Belhaven?"

"I hope it's not Milt's," Frances wailed. She burst into tears and buried her face in her hands.

Gloria reached over and wrapped her arm around Frances's shoulders. "I'm almost 100% certain it's not Milt," she assured her.

Frances shoved her chair back, grabbed her walker that was next to her chair and bolted from the room. Gloria's heart sank as she watched her shuffled from the room.

Liz chewed on the end of a French fry. "Nice going, sis," she said.

Gloria's head whipped around. She glared at Liz. "You didn't do much better." She mimicked her sister. "Did you hear about the body they found in Belhaven?"

Liz shrugged. Yeah. It probably wasn't the best choice in words to say to someone whose

174

love interest had just disappeared. "So how is the investigation going?"

Gloria shrugged. "Kind of at a standstill until they identify the body," she admitted.

Gloria told her who she thought it was and why. She changed the subject and they talked about Jill and the boys. Liz mentioned that her son, Eric, was coming for a visit. Eric lived somewhere out in Colorado. Gloria could never remember exactly where. He had a girlfriend that Liz had never met. "Is he bringing his girlfriend?"

"Casey?" Liz sawed off a piece of the liver on her plate and took a bite. "Yep. Finally get to meet her."

After they finished eating, the three of them wandered back to Liz's place. They chatted for a while and the conversation turned to the coins. "David said they're close to a decision and it's looking good."

Gloria tried not to get her hopes up. She didn't want to be disappointed if the courts ruled in the state's favor. She glanced at her watch. "We better go. I want to get home before dark."

Liz walked her to the door. "How's it going with Al?" Gloria asked as she grabbed the door handle.

Liz blushed. Her eyes slid to the ground. "Pretty good," she answered vaguely.

"Hmm." Gloria nodded. She didn't press the issue.

Gloria and Mally strolled back to the car. She opened the door for Mally then slid into the driver's seat before heading back to Belhaven.

Dot's dinner rush was over and only a couple cars were parked out front. For a split second, Gloria thought about stopping but drove on instead.

She needed a good night's rest what with the boys coming the next day. Mally and Gloria headed inside and settled in to watch Gloria's favorite TV show, *Detective on the Side.*

After the show ended, she wandered off to bed with Mally and Puddles in tow. She switched off the light and slid in between the sheets. Mally crawled in on the other side and Puddles curled up next to Gloria's head. She squeezed her eyes shut and began to pray, asking God for a restful night, certain that tomorrow was going to be a busy one!

Chapter 10

Gloria woke early the next morning. At first, her foggy brain couldn't register exactly *why* she was up so early, then it dawned on her. Her grandsons, Tyler and Ryan, were coming for a visit!

She flung back the covers, shoved her feet in her slippers and headed to the kitchen for a pot of caffeine.

Mally headed for the porch door and let out a low whine. It was time to go out.

Gloria pulled her robe tight and cinched the belt before stepping onto the porch. She smoothed her hair back and reached for the paper.

Smack dab on the front page of the morning paper was the headline: *"Bad Luck or Black Widow?"* Below the caption was a picture of Andrea's house with the dumpster off to the side.

Her heart sank. She hoped Andrea hadn't seen the paper – but chances are, she had.

She and Mally wandered into the house. Gloria set the paper on the table and poured a cup of coffee before sliding into a kitchen chair and slipping on her glasses. The article was brief. It told how another body – this one a skeleton – had been found in a dumpster out in front of the newly-renovated house. The article mentioned Andrea by name. How her husband had been found murdered and just weeks later, a body had been found in the shed on the property she had just purchased.

After she read the article, she folded the paper in half and shoved it to the back of the table. It did seem as if Andrea had the worst luck in the world. What were the chances of another body popping up on her property?

But each of those mysteries had been solved and Andrea had been cleared of all charges.

She wondered if Andrea's parents had read the paper. She also wondered how the dinner with Brian had gone the night before. She didn't have to wonder long.

Her kitchen phone started to ring. "Hello?"

"Did you see this morning's paper?" It was Andrea.

"Yes! And it's bunch of bull hockey!"

Andrea let out a deep sigh. "I guess I should be used to it by now."

"Don't let it get to you, Andrea. We both know someone put that body there and it wasn't you!"

Andrea lowered her voice. "My dad is fit to be tied." She went on. "He's on my computer right now, looking for apartments for me in New York."

Gloria's heart sunk. Had her parents finally convinced her to move? Gloria couldn't blame her if she was tired of all the drama.

"I've decided I am not moving," Andrea said stubbornly. "This is my home!"

"They're just trying to look out for your best interest," Gloria soothed. "Be firm but kind." She was glad to see Andrea's determination. She would need it to not only survive her parent's visit, but also muddle through another mystery.

"I will," Andrea promised. She changed the subject. "Hey! Remember the boxes in the attic? I found a small journal inside one of them. It was tucked in the very bottom."

A journal. Gloria's heart started to pound. "Did you look at it?"

Andrea shook her head, as if Gloria could see her through the phone. "Nope. I'm saving it for you. You want to come by later and pick it up?"

Gloria remembered the boys. "Tyler and Ryan will be here around lunchtime," she warned.

"Oh. You can bring them with you."

Gloria wasn't sure about that. Andrea was used to the boys being around - but the Thorntons? That was another story. "What about your parents?"

"They're going to be out this afternoon to run errands and such."

"Okay. We'll be there around 2 then."

Gloria poured another cup of coffee before heading to the bathroom to get ready for what was shaping up to be a very busy day.

After she showered and dressed, Mally and Gloria headed out onto the porch to wait for Jill and the boys. They had just settled in when Jill's car pulled in the drive. She could see the boys' heads bobbing up and down in the back seat.

She grinned as she watched the car come to a halt. The rear doors flung wide open and the boys raced each other to the porch. They both made it to the top at the same time. She wrapped an arm around each of them, pulling them close.

She beamed over their heads as her daughter made her way up the sidewalk, backpacks in hand. "They were driving me nuts! If they had their way, they'd have been here at six this morning. You would've thought it was Christmas or something."

Jill leaned over and kissed her mother's cheek. "Thanks for letting them stay."

The boys let go of Gloria and chased Mally into the yard. Jill followed her mother inside. She dropped the backpacks in the bedroom. "I'll run back out and get lunch. I hope Mexican is okay."

Gloria nodded. She loved Mexican. Sometimes it didn't love *her* so much, which was one of the reasons she didn't eat it often. She told her daughter the truth. "I love Mexican."

"Good." Jill headed to the car while Gloria cleared the kitchen table.

Tyler made it into the kitchen first. He pulled out a chair and plopped down. Ryan flung himself in the seat next to his brother.

Jill set the bags of food on the table and turned to her young sons. "Uh-uh. Go wash up first."

"Oh, man!" The boys hung their heads and headed to the bathroom.

Jill pulled the wrapped food from the bag. "Tacos, burritos and quesadillas."

Gloria's mouth watered. It all sounded good. All she'd eaten for breakfast was a slice of toast.

The boys were back from the bathroom and had plunked down into the chairs, watching as their mother set the food on the table.

Gloria unwrapped her bean burrito and laid it on top of the wrapper. She reached for a packet of hot sauce.

Ryan reached out and touched Gloria's finger. "That's a pretty ring, Grams."

Gloria glanced down at the sparkling sapphire.

Jill paused. "What ring?"

Gloria dropped her hand and flashed the sapphire and diamond ring at her daughter, who raised her eyebrows. "This is from Paul?"

Gloria's cheeks warmed and she nodded.

"Is that a wedding ring?" Tyler asked innocently.

Gloria shook her head. "No, Tyler. It's not a wedding ring."

"But it could be," Ryan added.

"Yes, it could be," Gloria admitted. "But it's not." She quickly changed the subject. "Did you hear about the skeleton in the dumpster over at Andrea's place?"

Jill smeared a glob of sour cream on top of her quesadilla and lifted it to her lips. "Yeah!" She shook her head. "Poor Andrea has the worst luck!"

"You found another body, Grams?" Tyler eyed his grandmother.

"Yes, Tyler. There was a body. An old body – in the dumpster by Andrea's house."

His eyes widened like saucers. "Do you think she has ghosts there, too?"

She shook her head. "No. There are no ghosts," she assured him. She looked up at Jill. "I have to run by her place later to pick something up."

Jill nodded. She finished her food, crumpled her wrappers and tossed them back into the food bag. "What time do you want me to pick the boys up tomorrow?"

"Never!" Ryan told his mother.

Gloria reached over and ruffled his blonde hair. "You don't want your mom to cry now, do you?"

He hung his head. "No." He lifted his eyes. "It's just that Gram's place has all the fun stuff." Then he remembered something his grandmother had promised him last time he'd stayed over. "Are you going to let us drive the tractor?"

His eyes pleaded with her. Gloria did not have the heart to tell him no – plus she *had* promised. "A promise is a promise," she answered.

"Yippee!! Ryan bounced out of his chair and danced a little jig around the kitchen. Gloria was a little nervous but assured herself it would be fine. *After all, what could possibly happen?*

They cleared the table and picked up their mess before Gloria walked Jill to the car. The boys had darted off to the garden.

Jill slipped her sunglasses on and opened the car door. "You sure about the tractor?"

"Yes. We'll just wander around the field," she told her. She sounded more confident than she felt. It was times like this she wished James were here. He could teach the boys to drive the tractor. But he wasn't and she was.

She watched as Jill pulled out of the drive and onto the road. She wandered over to the boys. "I'm going to quick run inside and grab my purse, then we're going over to Andrea's," she told them.

Neither of them looked up so she wasn't sure if they even heard her. She let Mally back in the house and grabbed her keys off the hook. The three of them climbed in the car and out of the drive. She smiled as she listened to the conversation in the back seat.

"I'm going to search the house for more bodies," Ryan informed his older brother.

"Ryan, there aren't any more bodies. Grams found them all," Tyler explained.

Gloria covered her mouth and grinned. She shook her head. Kids could say the darndest things. She wished she had a way to record some of the stuff that came out of their mouths!

Gloria pulled in the drive. She was relieved to see only Andrea's car.

The boys hopped out of the back seat and raced to the shed. In search of a body, Gloria decided. She cupped her hands to her mouth. "Don't leave the yard," she yelled.

Andrea swung the door open when Gloria hit the front porch. "I hope the boys are okay in the yard," she fretted.

Andrea craned her neck and looked off to the side. "Yeah! They can't hurt anything out there," she assured her.

Gloria followed Andrea into the house and down the hall to the kitchen. The first thing

Gloria noticed was the clutter in the new bar area, which was unusual for Andrea. She was very tidy. Everything had a place.

The second thing Gloria noticed was what was on the counter. There must've been a dozen containers of Lysol wipes, all lined up in a row. In front of the wipes were several unopened bags of surgical masks and next to that, a box of latex gloves.

Andrea followed Gloria's stare. She rolled her eyes. "My mother has sanitized every square inch of the house." She paused. "No. I take that back." She looked up at her kitchen ceiling. "She hasn't started up there yet."

Gloria leaned forward and ran her hand along a kitchen wall. "You mean to tell me she wiped all the walls with disinfecting wipes?"

Andrea reached up, grabbed a chunk of her long hair and pulled. "I'm ready to rip my hair out. Literally!"

The look on Andrea's face was too much. Gloria couldn't help herself. She burst out laughing.

The laughter was infectious. Soon, both women doubled over at the vision of Andrea's mother wiping the entire house down with Lysol.

Andrea wiped her eyes. "Oh, man. I needed that!" She rubbed her stomach. "Now my stomach hurts. It's all your fault!"

Gloria reached over and hugged her young friend. "You're a good daughter, Andrea. Your parents are lucky to have you," she told her.

Andrea reached back, rummaging around in the stacks of stuff. "Oh! Here! Before I forget!" She pulled out a small journal and handed it to Gloria. "This is what I found in the bottom of one of the boxes."

Gloria reached in her purse and grabbed her glasses. She slipped them on. The journal was old. On the front was a small, square frame.

Surrounding the frame were miniature flowering buds. Inside the picture part was another painting, similar to the ones they had found in the box. She opened the cover to inspect the front page.

Just then, Ryan burst through the back door. "Grams! Come quick!"

Gloria dropped the journal on the counter and raced out the back door. Andrea was hot on her heels.

Ryan raced over to the shed. The door was open and Gloria could see Tyler inside, bent over and staring at something. As they got closer, she could see a large piece of wood propped up against one of the cabinets.

Tyler pointed to the ground as the girls approached. "What's that?"

Gloria and Andrea peered in the door and followed his finger. There, lying in the dirt, was what looked like a burlap bag. Near the top of the bag was a large, dark splotch. Gloria leaned in. Lying on top of the bag was a long, thin stick.

She turned to Ryan. "Run inside and grab a glove from the kitchen counter," she told him.

He nodded his head and raced to the house. Moments later, he returned with a glove.

She stepped into the shed and tiptoed along the side of the wooden flooring until she was directly in front of the dark spot and the stick. She leaned in and with a gloved hand; she picked up the stick and held it to the light. It wasn't a stick at all. It looked like an old barn nail.

She glanced over at Andrea. "We should put this stuff in a trash bag. I'll take it to Paul." Andrea nodded. She headed back in the house for a trash bag while Gloria carefully folded the burlap bag and carried it out of the shed.

Andrea opened the garbage bag. Gloria dropped the nail in the bag first and the burlap bag on top. Andrea sealed the bag shut and set it next to the house.

They headed back to the shed for another look around. Tyler was standing outside the door now. He turned to his grandmother. "Did you see anything else?" she asked.

"Nope." He shook his head.

"How did you think to lift that board?" Andrea wondered.

Tyler shrugged his shoulders. "I dunno. We were running around the shed and then we decided to see if we could find more bodies inside like the time you and Grams found one."

Ryan interrupted. "And the floor was really creaky so I pulled on the board." He flung his hand in the air. "It popped up just like that."

Andrea shifted her gaze when she heard tires on the gravel drive. Her parents were back.

Gloria tapped Tyler's shoulder. "Go inside and wash your hands," she told them.

Andrea headed to the front to greet her parents while Gloria tucked the garbage bag behind a bush and out of sight. *No sense in giving Andrea's parents even more ammunition to convince her to move back to New York*, she decided.

She headed up the back steps and into the kitchen. When she opened the door, she spied Ryan standing next to the counter. He had pulled one of Libby Thornton's surgical masks from the bag and was now wearing it.

Her eyes darted to Tyler. He was wearing a pair of the surgical gloves. "C'mon. Let's go operate on Brutus," Tyler told his brother.

"You need to..." Before Gloria could get the words "take those off!" out of her mouth, Andrea and her parents rounded the corner and entered the kitchen, coming face-to-face with Tyler and Ryan.

Libby's eyes widened. Her hand flew to her mouth. "What on earth..."

Gloria snatched the mask from Ryan's face and the gloves from Tyler's hands simultaneously.

Libby's eyes narrowed, her lips thinned. She shoved her hand on her hip. "And just *who* are *you?*" Her eyes were boring holes – first into Ryan, then Tyler.

Gloria stepped forward. "I'm sorry. These are my grandsons. They didn't mean any harm."

Libby stomped over and grabbed the mask that Ryan had just had on and the gloves that Tyler had been wearing. She marched over to the trash can and tossed them inside. "You have contaminated my perfectly-sterile items!"

Andrea walked over to the trash can. "Now, Mom. They're just boys. They didn't hurt anything."

Libby whirled around, her eyes like 4th of July firecrackers. She glared at Gloria. "They should be taught manners. Something they're obviously lacking," she hissed.

Gloria put a protective hand on the boys' shoulders. She ignored the wrath of Libby and turned to Andrea. "We should be going now. I'll talk to you later."

Without waiting for a reply, Gloria and the boys headed out the back door and down the steps.

"That lady is mean," Ryan told Gloria.

"Yeah. We were just playing," Tyler piped up.

"I know, boys. It's okay."

Tyler turned sorrowful eyes to his beloved Grams. "You think we have manners, don't you, Grams?"

Gloria felt her blood begin to boil. There was no reason for Andrea's mother to go off like that!

It was a flimsy surgical mask and a cheap pair of gloves! The stupid things couldn't have cost more than a couple bucks!

She was still fuming as she snapped her seat belt in place and started the car. It took her until she was almost back at the farm before she calmed down. She was certain of one thing. She would *not* be visiting Andrea again until her parents left!

Chapter 11

The boys flung open the car doors and raced each other across the drive and into the house. Gloria followed them in. She dropped her keys and purse on the table and glanced over at the answering machine. The light was flashing. She pressed the button. It was Andrea. "Gloria, I am so sorry! My mother doesn't normally act that way. Can you please tell the boys I'm sorry?"

Gloria could tell by her voice she was near tears. "They're leaving in the morning," she whispered. "I'll call you after they're gone."

The boys had already forgotten about mean-old Libby. They were ready to ride the tractor. Gloria compromised. "Go play in the barn for a little while and I'll be out in less than an hour," she promised.

After they scampered out into the yard, she picked up her cell phone to call Paul. She wanted to tell him what the boys had found in the shed.

"Forensics should have the results back in the morning," he told her. "I'll stop by later to pick those things up."

Gloria glanced out the window. The boys had opened the barn door. *They must be inside*, she thought. "Great. Maybe you'll make it in time to watch me show the boys how to drive the old tractor."

"Wouldn't miss that for the world." He chuckled. "I'll be there in an hour," he promised.

After they hung up, Gloria decided to wait until he got there. It might be a good idea to have someone around just in case something went wrong...

She slipped on her yard shoes and headed outside to check on the boys. The barn was quiet. Too quiet. She looked around. "Ryan? Tyler?" Nothing. A sudden motion caught her eye. She looked up.

The boys had managed to climb into the tractor and were sitting behind the wheel. They waved at Gloria when they saw her. She waved back.

Tyler opened the door and leaned out. "Can we drive it now?"

She shook her head. "We're going to wait for Paul to come over," she told them.

His eyelids drooped and he shoved his chin on his fist.

"It shouldn't be long," she promised. "Why don't you see what you can find left in the garden while we're waiting?"

That seemed to make both boys happy. They scrambled out of the tractor and raced across the yard. Mally was right behind them, her tongue hanging out of her mouth as she chased them to the garden.

Gloria wandered back into the house. In all the excitement, she'd completely forgotten about the journal that Andrea had found in the box. She plucked it from her purse, opened the closet door and placed it on an upper shelf - safe and sound from little hands that might decide there was a better use for the old book than to read it.

She closed the closet door and watched as Paul's unmarked police car pulled in. Her heart skipped a beat and she glanced down at the ring. A small smile reached her lips as she headed outside and over to the car.

She shoved her hands in the front pockets of her capris and leaned back to watch as he climbed out. "Howdy stranger."

He grinned, grabbed her arm and started to pull her close. "Careful of the little eyes watching," she warned.

Paul glanced over at the garden. "Whoops! I almost forgot!" He gave her a quick peck on the lips and let go of her hand.

The boys spied Paul and darted over to the car. "So now we get to drive the tractor?" Tyler asked.

Gloria slowly nodded. Her word was her word. "Yes, now is the time."

Paul smacked his hands together and rubbed them in glee. "This I have to see!"

The four of them made their way over to the open barn doors. "You stay out here until I get the tractor out of the barn," she told them. She didn't wait for a reply as she stepped into the barn and hoisted herself up the three metal steps that led to the cab door.

She opened the door and slipped inside. The keys were in the ignition. She never bothered to take them out but now that the boys were learning to drive it, she made a mental note to keep them in the house after today.

The tractor fired up on the first try. She pressed down on the clutch and shifted into low gear. The tractor lurched forward and slowly rolled out of the barn. When the tractor cleared the barn doors, she slipped it into neutral and put both feet on the brake.

She decided it was best to take them one at a time. She pushed the door open and motioned for Ryan to climb up first. He clambered up the steps and scooched into the small cab. "Where do I sit, Grams?"

The seat was small - really only large enough for one person. "You'll have to sit here on my lap," she told him. He nodded and climbed into her lap then grabbed the steering wheel.

Paul and Tyler stepped to the side as Gloria took her foot off the brake, pressed in the clutch and put it in the lowest gear possible. The tractor jerked forward and began a slow crawl across the yard. She let out the breath she'd been holding. Since Ryan was younger, he was happy with the slow meandering.

"Steer to the right," she told him.

Ryan grabbed the wheel with both hands and pulled. They slipped in between the garden and the garage as they headed toward the open fields back behind the barn.

They chugged over to one of the harvested fields. The tilled earth was a bit bumpy. The tractor wandered up and down the field. Back and forth for several trips.

Ryan jerked his head around, his small hands holding tight to the wheel. "Can we go any faster, Grams?"

Gloria nodded. She didn't see the harm in moving the tractor into the next higher gear. She glanced around. The coast was clear.

She inched it into second gear and they bounced along the rutted field, which Ryan thought was hilarious. Every time they hit a bump and lifted off the seat, he burst into a fit of giggles.

Gloria wished she had a camera to capture the moment. The look of sheer joy on his face was priceless. They rode back and forth several more times before she told him it was Tyler's turn. Gloria was certain her oldest grandson was chomping at the bit.

They circled around the drive and stopped in the same spot they had started.

Ryan climbed out and Tyler climbed in. Tyler was taller than his younger brother was. Soon he would be taller than Gloria. Even now, there was no way he could fit on her lap.

She scooched to the edge and motioned him to sit beside her. They both teetered on the outer edge of the narrow cushion as Gloria once again slipped the tractor into gear and the two of them headed for the field.

Tyler was much more impatient than his younger brother was and first gear wasn't fast enough. "We're barely moving," he complained.

Since Ryan had managed in second gear, Gloria didn't hesitate to move it up a notch, which seemed to make him happy for a few minutes. "One more speed higher, Grams. I can do it," his bright eyes begged.

Her eyebrows furrowed as she studied her grandson. They were still a safe distance from any sort of objects so she nodded her head and moved the gear up one more. The tractor jostled up and down. Gloria felt as if she was bouncing up and down on a pogo stick. It was beginning to make her dizzy. "We better slow it down and head back." *Before I throw up,* she thought to herself.

She shifted the tractor down a gear and Tyler steered the tractor towards the house. They were close to the spot where they had started. Everything was going fine until Tyler decided it would be great fun to jerk the wheel in Mally's direction and chase her down with the tractor.

With a look of determination on his face, he set his mouth in a straight line and zeroed in on Gloria's beloved pooch. Mally saw the tractor turn and darted out of its path.

"Tyler!"

It was as if he didn't hear Gloria as he jerked the wheel again and they careened past the garden, once again bearing down on poor Mally!

She gave a quick glance in Paul and Ryan's direction. She could see the fear in their eyes as they ran behind the large oak tree, a safe distance from the tractor-gone-wild.

Gloria did the only thing she could think to do. She slid down in the seat and jammed her foot on the clutch. She grabbed the steering wheel with one hand and twisted her body to the side. With her other hand, she switched the ignition to the "off" position. The tractor came to a screeching halt.

Tyler jerked forward, his chest hitting the center of the wheel. His eyes slid to the side, as he peeked over at his grandmother. One look and he knew he was in big trouble.

Gloria opened her mouth but it was too late. Tyler had jerked the cabin door open and jumped to the ground.

Gloria gave him a dark look before she started the tractor and slowly backed it into the barn. She was still upset as she climbed out of the tractor, the keys clenched tightly in her fist.

She marched over to her eldest grandson. She opened her mouth to let him have it.

Tyler lowered his head. "Sorry, Grams. I don't know what came over me," he confessed. "I got carried away."

She stuck one hand on her hip and ran the other through her frazzled hair. "*Carried away*? You could've hurt Mally, young man! Or us," she added

Paul opened his mouth to speak but quickly closed it. He wisely decided it was probably best if he not get into the middle of this one.

"On top of that, you scared me half to death! My life flashed before my very eyes." That part was a bit of an exaggeration, but he had scared her.

She lifted her hand and shook her finger at him. "Just for that, the next time you come over, Ryan gets to drive the tractor but you don't," she told him.

Tyler hung his head and shuffled his feet as he made his way up to the house. Ryan and Paul followed quietly behind.

By the time they were inside, Gloria had cooled off a bit. She found Tyler lying on the bed, staring at the ceiling. She sat down on the edge of the bed. "I'm done being angry."

"I shouldn't have done that," he admitted.

"No, you shouldn't have," she agreed. "But it's over now so we'll put it behind us."

His head whipped around to face his grandmother. "So that means I can drive the tractor next time I'm here?"

"Nope." She shook her head firmly. "You lost that privilege for now."

She leaned forward and kissed his forehead before heading back to the kitchen. Tyler followed her out.

She reached into the pantry and pulled out a Tupperware container. "I made brownies the other day. Who's hungry?"

"Me!" replied three male voices in unison. The group settled in at the table with four large glasses of milk and a container full of brownies that quickly vanished.

The boys headed back outside as Gloria cleaned the dish and put it back in the cupboard. Paul helped by rinsing the dirty glasses and putting them in the dishwasher. "You have that bag of stuff you found out at Andrea's place?"

Gloria wiped her hands on the towel and hung it on the front of the stove. The bag was still in the trunk of her car.

"I'll be right back." She wandered out to Annabelle and pulled the garbage bag from the trunk. Paul met her on the porch. She handed him the bag and sat down on the rocker. She watched while he untied the bag and peered inside. "Tell me again where you found this."

"The boys found it." Gloria went on to explain how the boys were playing out in the shed and remembered when Andrea and Gloria had found the first body.

That the boys decided to search for more when they lifted the floorboards that were loose and found the burlap bag spread out on the dirt.

He pulled the drawstrings and turned the bag for a better look.

She jumped up from her chair. "Here, let me get a glove." She ran out to the garage and grabbed a pair of gardening gloves she kept on the small bench near the door.

When she returned, she handed him the gloves and sat back down.

He reached into the garbage bag and pulled out what Gloria thought looked like a nail. He turned it over in his hand. "This looks like an old nail."

She nodded. "That's what I thought. An old roofing or barn nail."

He set the nail on the table before reaching back in and pulling out the burlap. He grabbed the top corners and held it out for inspection. "That sure does look like some kind of stain." He glanced back at Gloria. "Wouldn't that be something if it matched the DNA on the skeleton in the dumpster?"

Gloria nodded. She wouldn't bet her life on it, but she had a strong hunch the two were connected.

Paul put the two items back in the bag and pulled the drawstrings. He pulled the gloves off and laid them on the table before leaning back in the rocker. "Paul and Tina are gone."

She smiled. "I'm glad. For everyone's sake."

"Me too. Although it's mighty quiet around the house now," he admitted. "Except for Dorito. He's quite a stinker."

Gloria's eyes scanned the yard and came to rest on the boys who were out near the barn. She shook her head. "Good grief!"

Paul followed her gaze and then burst out laughing. Mally was sitting upright inside the wheelbarrow. Tyler was pushing her around the yard. She looked happy as a clam, her tongue hanging out as air blew back tufts of brown fur. "What those boys don't think of."

"You should bring them over sometime. They can run through the cornfields out back before they harvest it."

She nodded. The boys would love to run through the cornfields.

Paul reluctantly got to his feet and reached over to pick up the garbage bag. "I better get this down to the lab so they can put a rush on it."

She nodded and pulled herself from the chair. She was eager to find out what was up with the bag. Which reminded her of something else. "Did they find anything out on that painting?"

Paul snapped his fingers. "I'm glad you reminded me." He shook his head. "Nothing came up so Andrea can have it back. It's in the trunk."

She followed him to the car and waited while he popped the trunk and pulled out the portrait. Gloria grabbed the jagged edge, careful not to touch the painting itself. "Margaret has a friend who owns an art gallery down in Grand Rapids. We're going to take it there to see what he can tell us about it."

Paul opened the car door and leaned on the edge. Gloria looked past the car. Mally was out of the wheelbarrow now. The boys were holding sticks in their hands and poking at something on the ground.

She leaned forward and popped up on her tippy-toes. Paul leaned down and kissed her on the lips. "Someday we won't have to sneak kisses," he promised.

"Grams! Come quick!" Ryan was waving frantically in her direction.

She sighed. "I better go. 'Come quick!' is code word for 'we got into something we probably shouldn't have.'"

Paul grinned and slid into the driver's seat. He gave her a small wave before pulling out of the drive.

Gloria hustled over to where the boys and Mally were circled around. She bent over and looked down. "What have you found now?"

There, on the ground, was a small pile of arrowheads. "How did you find these?"

Tyler shuffled his tennis shoe across the loose dirt. "I was thinking about climbing this tree." Tyler pointed up. "When I got underneath this branch, I saw something shiny so I picked it up," he explained.

"Then we started digging around and found more," Ryan chimed in.

Gloria plucked an arrowhead from the pile and held it up in the sunlight. She had never found arrowheads on the farm before. Of course, she knew that Chippewa Indians had once roamed the area.

"Can we keep 'em?" Ryan asked.

"Yes, of course." Gloria turned the sharp stone over in her hand. "Try not to stab each other with them."

The boys spent a few more minutes digging around before pocketing the ten arrowheads they had found.

With their treasures tucked safely away in their pockets, she gave them a gentle nudge towards the house. "Go wash up so we can eat," she told them.

She followed them in and made a beeline for the fridge. Nothing inside looked the least bit appealing. She opened the freezer door. Inside was a packet of frozen hamburger meat and that was about it. She shut the door as the boys wandered back into the kitchen. "Let's head down to Dot's for dinner."

Ryan lifted his right leg and hopped in a circle. He licked his lips and rubbed his stomach. "I already know what I'm gonna get," he informed his grandmother. "A cheeseburger and fries and a chocolate shake and a piece of pie."

Gloria shook her head. "The cheeseburger and fries – yes. The sweets - no. You already ate an entire pan of brownies," she reminded him.

Gloria grabbed her purse and keys. They hopped in the car and drove to town. The dinner crowd was in full swing as Gloria and the boys headed indoors and over to one of the few remaining booths. The boys slid in one side while Gloria took the other.

Gloria already knew what she wanted. She was going to order the pot roast. She had been planning to make some herself but hadn't gotten around to it. The boys didn't bother picking up the menus either.

Dot appeared at the table with three glasses of water in hand. "If it isn't Tyler and Ryan." She glanced at Gloria. "I didn't know the boys were coming over." Gloria slid her straw from the paper wrapper. She tapped the ice cubes to the side and dropped the straw in the glass. "It was kind of spur-of-the-moment."

"We're starving," Ryan informed Dot.

Dot smiled. "You do look mighty hungry. Hungry enough to eat a bear," she teased.

"Or an elephant," he added.

Dot jotted down their order and headed to the back. Gloria relented just a fraction on the sweets. She let them both order a root beer. The ones that came in the frosted mugs.

Margaret and her husband, Don, walked in moments later. She waved at Gloria then pulled on her husband's arm. Don smiled at Gloria and the boys. "I'll grab that booth before someone else gets it." He didn't wait for an answer as he headed to a booth a couple spots away.

Margaret watched his retreating back before turning to Gloria. "How's Andrea doing?" she asked. "Her parents are the hot gossip in town. I heard they came in here for lunch and her mother was wearing some sort of mask."

Gloria bristled. Just the thought of Libby Thornton made her mad. The woman was not a nice person.

Margaret caught the look. "So I take it you don't care for them," she surmised.

Tyler grabbed the bottle of ketchup on the far end of the table. He popped the top off, tipped his head back and squirted a glob in his mouth. "She yelled at us."

Margaret raised her eyebrows. "Really?"

Gloria briefly explained how the boys had gotten into her supply of masks and gloves and she had thrown a fit. "I guess they're leaving soon."

Margaret shook her head. "Poor Andrea. She never seems to get a break."

"Grams found a body in Andrea's dumpster," Ryan told Margaret.

She nodded. "I heard." She turned to Gloria. "Any news?"

She shook her head. "Tomorrow. Paul said the results would be back from the lab tomorrow."

"And Andrea has a secret hiding spot under her shed," Ryan added.

Don was motioning Margaret over to the table. Dot was standing next to him, trying to take their order. "I better go order." She gave Gloria a hard look. "I'll call you later."

They were still waiting for their food to arrive when Ruth popped in. She was alone. Gloria waved her over and slid across the vinyl bench seat to make room.

Ruth looked over at Tyler and Ryan. "Well, if it isn't two of my favorite boys in the whole wide world!"

Ruth had a chance to get to know the boys when she'd stayed at Gloria's house not long ago. At first, Gloria thought they might get on her nerves since she never had children of her own and wasn't used to having them around. But the boys had taken a liking to Ruth and she seemed to enjoy them just as much.

"We got to drive the tractor," Ryan told Ruth.

Ruth drummed the top of the table with her nails. She dropped her chin in her hand. "I bet that was fun!"

"Let's just say it was an adventure," Gloria muttered.

Ruth chuckled and shook her head. "I wish I'd been there to see it."

Ryan chugged his root beer, which left a foamy moustache on his upper lip. He wiped it off with the back of his hand. "Tyler tried to run over Mally."

Tyler punched his brother in the arm. "I did not!"

Gloria raised her eyebrows at her grandson. "That's enough."

He crossed his arms and leaned his head back against the seat. "At least not on purpose," he pouted.

Dot was headed their way with a tray full of food. Gloria felt bad about eating in front of Ruth. She needn't have worried. Dot must've noticed Ruth sitting there. She brought an extra plate. This one filled with fried chicken, a scoop of mashed potatoes, minus the gravy, a side of corn and a freshly baked roll.

Ruth's mouth fell open. She stared up at her friend. "How did you know I was going to order this?"

Dot tapped her pen against the pad of paper in her hand. "A wild guess."

But that wasn't really the truth. The girls had been friends for decades - so long that they could almost read each other's minds. Gloria wasn't sure if that was a good thing – or a bad thing.

Dot disappeared in the back while the four of them enjoyed a leisurely dinner, chatting about this and that. Gloria wrapped a few chunks of her meat in a paper napkin and slipped it into her purse.

"Mally likes Dot's cooking," Tyler told Ruth.

Ryan shoved a whole fry in his mouth and eyed his brother. "Puddles, too."

Ruth nodded. "I bet they both like pot roast. I don't know anyone that doesn't, especially Dot's."

Gloria finished her final few bites of baked potato. "Hear anything at the post office about the skeleton?"

Ruth was almost always one of the first people to hear the gossip in town. Not that she minded. Ruth loved to keep up on all the residents. She was like a modern-day town crier. "Nope. It's been very quiet." She paused as she sipped her ice water. "Very odd."

Gloria remembered the journal tucked away in the cupboard. She planned take a peek at it tonight, after the boys were in bed. If she wasn't too tired. Today had been a busy one.

The girls took their bills to the cash register to pay. When they were finished, they stopped by Margaret's table. Margaret and Don had ordered the fried chicken, too. Margaret laid the piece on her plate and wiped her hands on the napkin in her lap. "This is some of the best chicken I have ever tasted."

Dot was coming up behind them to refill their drinks. "You think so?"

"Absolutely!" Gloria declared. "Ruth shared a piece with me and now I'm sorry I didn't order it!"

"Why, I'd pay twice as much for it," Ruth chimed in.

Dot turned a tint of pink. "You're not just saying that because you're my best friends."

Tyler grabbed Gloria's hand. "Grams is one of the best cooks on the whole planet. If she said it's good – it's gotta be good!"

They all laughed at Tyler's declaration before heading out the door. Ruth stopped near the front. "I heard something about a locked door in Andrea's basement." She shuddered. "What do you think might be inside?"

Gloria shook her head. She had no idea, but she had every intention of finding out!

Chapter 12

Gloria tucked the boys into bed and listened to their prayers. Mally curled up on the rug between the twin beds as Gloria quietly closed the door, leaving it open just a crack in case the boys needed her during the night.

She pulled the small journal from its hiding place and took it into the bedroom with her.

She changed into her pajamas and climbed into bed. Puddles sprang up onto the bed and the two of them settled in for a bit of reading.

Gloria slid her glasses on and flipped the switch on the reading lamp she kept clamped to her headboard.

She opened the front cover. Inside was the neatly handwritten name *Barbara Johnson*. Gloria's pulse raced. The journal belonged to Abe's wife! Gloria turned to the first page.

"Today was uneventful. Boring if truth be told...."

Gloria had to agree with the first entry. The journal was full of rambling thoughts on her life in a small town and the day-in, day-out grind of living there. It was so boring Gloria started to nod off.

She glanced at her alarm clock. It was getting late. She decided to read one final page before turning in.

"I spent most of the day painting on the back patio. The skies were perfect light to finish my latest work. I decided to title it 'Fallen at Sunset.' I fear this isn't my best work, but it has become one of my favorites."

The journal went on. *"It's such a pity that the world will no longer be able to enjoy my works as they have in the past. But Abe insists I forget about presenting my work to the world. His jealousy is sometimes too much.*

Now that his stepbrother, Hank, is here, it has gotten even worse. I spend most evenings in my room to avoid arguing.

It is with great regret I say that the famous artist, Sofia Masson, is forever gone."

Gloria closed the journal and set it on her nightstand. Her head was spinning. *Abe Johnson's wife, Barbara, had been a famous painter?*

She thought about the small paintings that Andrea and she had found in the box. Gloria now had another question ping ponging around in her brain. *If this woman had been a famous painter, where were her paintings?*

Chapter 13

The boys were up bright and early the next morning. They flung Gloria's bedroom door open and jumped on the bed. Puddles, still curled up next to Gloria's head, took one look at the boys and sprung from the bed in one quick movement. Apparently, he still had not forgotten the time the boys tried to give him a bath in the toilet bowl.

Gloria threw back the covers and pulled on her robe. "Time for Gram's famous lumberjack breakfast," she told them.

Ryan jumped up and down on the bed. "I'm starving."

Gloria grabbed him 'round the waist and in one swift movement pulled him off. She tickled his ribs before letting him go. "I think you have a tapeworm, Ryan."

Ryan grabbed Gloria's hand as they followed Tyler into the kitchen. "And it eats ALL my food!"

The boys helped Gloria whip up a hearty breakfast of pancakes, sausage, eggs and toast. After they finished eating, the boys headed outdoors with Mally. Gloria looked around the kitchen. It looked like a tornado had touched down! She grabbed a dishrag and started to scrub the pile of dishes.

An hour later, the kitchen was shipshape. Gloria hung her apron on the hook and wandered out to check on the boys. The barn door was wide open but when she stuck her head inside, they were nowhere in sight.

She walked around the barn and into the garage. Still no sign of them. Her heart thumped. It was as if the boys had vanished into thin air!

She picked up the pace as she headed back to the porch. *Maybe they had gone back inside and she hadn't noticed*, she thought.

Her foot hit the bottom step when she heard the sound of laughter. It was coming from the front yard. Seconds later, Mally barked.

She spun around and headed to the front yard. In the middle of her front yard was a large, black walnut tree. Mally was beside it and she was looking up. *Woof!*

Gloria made her way over to Mally and looked up, too. There, several branches up in the tree were her grandsons.

It reminded her so much of the days her boys, Eddie and Ben, would climb the very same tree. Of course, back then the tree was smaller. A lump formed in her throat at the memory. She blinked back the unexpected tears. It seemed like just yesterday.

Tyler noticed Gloria first. "Hi Grams!" He waved. Gloria opened her mouth to tell them to get down but the memory of her own boys was so strong, she paused.

Kids these days were too sheltered. Not that Jill sheltered them. In her daughter's defense, they lived in town. Not on a big, old farm, full of things to keep young bodies and minds busy. No. Gloria wasn't going to tell them to come down.

"Hey Grams!" Ryan peeked his head from around a thick branch. "Can we build a tree fort?"

A tree fort. What a great idea! She slowly nodded. "Sure c'mon down and we'll see what we can find in the barn."

If Gloria wasn't mistaken, there was a stack of good-sized boards still in the barn. James had bought the boards years ago to repair some rotting floorboards in the shed.

The boys scampered out of the tree and raced to the barn. By the time Gloria caught up with them, they had pulled several pieces from the tidy pile she had stacked in the corner.

Tyler looked back when he heard Gloria's steps on the cement floor. "We need a hammer and nails," he said.

She nodded and headed for the garage – to James's old workbench - to gather what she thought they would need. When she got back, the boys had laid out several boards. She handed each of them a pair of James's work gloves. Her eyes filled with tears as she watched her grandsons slip on the familiar gloves.

How James would've loved to help the boys build a tree fort! She ran into the house and grabbed her camera. The boys were hard at work when she returned. They never even looked up as she snapped several photos of them hammering away at the boards.

Tyler got to his feet. He pulled the glove from his hand and wiped the sweat from his brow. "I'm thirsty."

"I'll go grab some drinks." She headed back inside, where she grabbed a couple bottled waters and some granola bars. She carried them back outside and the three of them sat on the hard cement floor to eat their snack. Gloria popped the top of the water and took a small sip. "You boys are doing a great job!"

Tyler took a large drink of his water and wiped his mouth with the back of his hand. "Thanks Grams."

"Thanks for letting us put it in the tree," Ryan chimed in. She ruffled his head and hugged his neck. "Thanks for building it. I can't wait to see what it looks like when it's done."

The boys got back to work and Gloria wandered to the porch. She settled into the rocker. Her heart swelled with pride as she watched the boys work on their masterpiece.

Finally, they ran across the yard, over to where Gloria was still sitting. "We're done with the floor," Ryan announced.

Gloria slid out of the chair and followed them to the barn. She stuck a hand on her hip and looked down at the wooden platform. They had done a dandy job, carefully matching the boards and making the frame square.

She bent down for a closer inspection. The frame was loaded with nails! Too many to count. She covered her mouth to hide her grin. Too many was better than not enough in her book!

"How are we going to get it up in the tree?" she wondered.

"I got an idea, Grams," Tyler replied. He walked over to the corner of the barn and grabbed a pile of braided ropes. "We can tie this around the boards and throw the one end over a branch to pull it up."

He didn't wait for an answer as he handed the rope to his younger brother and picked up the wooden frame with both hands. When they got to the tree, he took the rope from Ryan and tied it around the frame. The only suggestion Gloria could think to make was to tie a few extra knots.

Tyler nodded solemnly and took his grandmother's suggestion. He finished tightening the knots then flung one end of the rope around a sturdy branch. The end dangled down far enough for Ryan to reach. Tyler turned to his brother. "I'm going to go up first so I can grab it."

Ryan nodded.

Tyler turned to Gloria. "Grams is gonna have to help you pull the rope and lift the boards."

Tyler reminded Gloria of a monkey as he scrambled up the tree and settled back against a limb. He cupped his hands to his mouth. "Bring 'er up," he hollered down.

Ryan and Gloria grabbed the other end of the rope and started to pull. The rope held as they slowly inched the frame up and into the tree. When it got close, Tyler reached over and grabbed the boards. He swung it around and eased the platform into a flat section of the limbs. It was a perfect fit!

Gloria clapped her hands. "Good job boys!"

Tyler beamed with pride. He untied the rope and dropped it to the ground before climbing down. "Maybe we should tie it down. You know. So it doesn't wobble around and accidentally fall out."

"Great idea." She pointed to the rope in Ryan's hands. "You can use that."

Tyler turned to his brother and mumbled something. Ryan nodded and turned to face his grandmother. "Can we have a piece of cardboard and a marker?"

She nodded and headed inside for the two requested items. When she came back, she tossed them up and then left the boys to finish their project as she wandered over to the porch.

Her cell phone, which she had left on the side table by the rocker, was ringing. It was Andrea.

Gloria had left her a message earlier, telling her what she'd learned from the journal. "Hello dear."

"I got your message. So the woman that we thought was Barbara Johnson was really a famous painter?"

"That's what she wrote in the journal."

"But where are all the paintings?"

Gloria glanced at the door. "Paul dropped off the one that we found in the dumpster." She paused. "You don't think she hid the rest behind the walls?" That would mean Andrea would have to tear her house down just to find them...

No one in their right mind would do something crazy like that. "Maybe they're in the locked room in the basement?" Andrea wondered.

Gloria hoped that was not the case. The cold, damp basement would most certainly ruin the paintings.

Gloria heard a loud noise on Andrea's end. "What's that banging noise?"

"Oh! The construction crew. They're working on my sunroom."

"But isn't that going to aggravate your parents?"

"Nope! They left this morning." Andrea sounded downright giddy. "You've got to stop by and see the progress. It's going to be awesome. All glass walls. Saltillo tile floors."

"The boys will be leaving soon. I'll come by after that," Gloria promised.

She hung up the phone and stepped into the kitchen where she quickly whipped up a pile of tuna fish sandwiches and put them and a heaping mound of potato chips on the table. She headed out to find the boys. They were up in the fort.

Well, it wasn't technically a "fort" yet. It still needed walls, a roof and windows.

She shaded her eyes and peered up into the tree. *Maybe she could run down to the hardware store and have Brian cut a couple sheets of particleboard or plywood for her...*

"Time for lunch," she hollered up.

The boys scampered down the tree. "We need to finish the treehouse."

Gloria nodded. "After lunch you can measure the base. I'll have Brian down at the hardware store cut some walls with windows for you. Next time you're here you can finish building it," she promised.

Tyler's shoulders drooped. "You mean we can't finish it today?"

"I'm afraid not." The words were no more out of her mouth when Jill's car pulled in the drive.

Gloria waited for her to get out while the boys ran inside to wash up. When the girls got in the house, the boys were already eating.

Jill ruffled her youngest son's hair. "Did you have fun?"

Ryan spun around in the chair. "Yep! I got to drive the tractor, we found some arrowheads, and we found a secret compartment in Andrea's shed," he told his mother.

"And we started a tree fort," Tyler finished.

Ryan took a big bite of his sandwich. "Yeah! It's gonna be *AWESOME*!" he mumbled through his mouthful of food.

Jill smiled. "I can't wait to check it out."

The boys wolfed down their food. Ryan tugged on Jill's arm. "C'mon. You gotta see it."

Jill followed the boys to the front yard. They were already up in the tree and standing on the wooden frame.

Gloria headed to the garage for a tape measure. She stopped in the house for her reading glasses and piece of paper to jot down the measurements.

When she got back to the tree, she tossed the tape measure to Tyler and waited while the boys measured the frame.

It was then she noticed a piece of cardboard. The piece she had given them earlier. The boys had nailed it to the side of the tree. In bold, black letters was a warning:

"NO GIRLS ALLOWED. 'CEPT FOR GRAMS!"

Jill choked back her laughter. "I guess Tyler doesn't like girls. At least not yet!"

"'Cept for Grams," Gloria quoted. It reminded her of the Little Rascals and the "he man woman haters club."

Jill pulled her cell phone from her rear pocket. "Hey boys! Let me take a picture."

The boys scrambled to the edge of the frame and plopped down, their legs dangling over the side of the wooden frame.

Tyler stuck his arm around his younger brother's shoulder and grinned.

Jill snapped a couple quick shots. "Got it." She turned to her mother. "I'll send you a copy later," she said.

Gloria nodded. She knew exactly where she was putting the picture. On her computer screen saver so she could look at those handsome faces every day.

"I'm going to have Brian at the hardware store cut a couple pieces of plywood to build the walls." She watched as the boys headed back down. "You two go home and do some research on building a roof for the tree fort and then when you come back, we'll finish it," she told them.

Ryan impatiently brushed his blonde bangs out of his eyes and turned to Gloria. "Can we spend the night and sleep in it when it's done?"

That was a thought. Gloria eyes traveled to the half-built fort, then over to the screened-in front porch that ran the entire length of the front of the house. She *could* pull out the fold-up cot and sleep on the porch for one night. "We'll see."

After Jill and the boys left, Gloria grabbed the journal. She shoved it into her bag and headed for her car. She was anxious to see Andrea.

Gloria pulled into Andrea's drive. Her eyes wandered to the left hand side of the house – and the new sun porch.

Gloria slid out of the car and closed the door. It was bigger than she had envisioned. It was going to be beautiful.

She caught a glimpse of Andrea out back. She was watching the workers.

From what Gloria could tell, the only thing they had left to do was install a few more glass panels.

She wandered to the side and came up next to her young friend.

Andrea shaded her eyes. "Well. What do you think?"

"It's lovely, Andrea."

"Follow me."

Gloria followed Andrea around the construction zone and into the backyard where her flower garden was thriving. It was a rainbow of roses and tulips. The scent of the roses filled the air as Gloria followed Andrea down the path. "Your roses are stunning."

Andrea abruptly stopped. "I just love it out here. Imagine when the sunroom is finished and it overlooks the flower garden."

Gloria could hear the sound of water. She peeked around the edge of a blooming bush. There, sitting in the corner of the perfectly landscaped space, was a three-tier fountain. It was in the shape of a castle. An array of magnificent tulips surrounded it. "What a surprise."

They wandered back out front and over to Annabelle. Gloria pulled the painting from the trunk and handed it to Andrea. "I did some research on the painter, Sofia Masson."

Gloria slammed the trunk shut. "And?"

"She was a famous French painter who pretty much disappeared off the face of the earth. Mysteriously vanished is how the article described it."

Andrea looked down at the painting. "There was a small photo of her. I think this is a self-portrait."

She led Gloria back inside the house and propped the painting against a dining room wall. Gloria looked past the living room and into the new sun porch. The French doors leading to the sunroom were wide open. "I can't wait to see it finished."

"C'mon." Andrea and Brutus headed down the small hall and into the kitchen. Gone were the rows of Lysol wipes and boxes of gloves. She pulled out a barstool near the counter and motioned Gloria to have a seat.

Gloria eased onto the seat and pulled the journal from her purse. She flipped it open and then pushed it towards Andrea. "Here's the journal entry I told you about."

Andrea quickly read the words. "That's amazing," she said.

Gloria hadn't had time to finish reading. There wasn't much left to read. Just a few more entries. "Would you like a Coke?"

Gloria nodded. "We should finish the journal together."

Andrea popped the top on a can she pulled from the fridge and handed it to Gloria. "In the library."

The library was one of Gloria's favorite parts of the house. When she had some extra time, she planned to investigate it thoroughly. Andrea settled into one of the comfy cushioned chairs and Gloria plopped down on the other.

Andrea sipped her soda and set the can on a coaster nearby. "Did I tell you Alice is coming to live with me?"

Gloria looked up from the journal. "You mentioned that she might."

Andrea nodded. "Yep. She's packing up now."

Gloria remembered Andrea telling her that Alice hated New York. Hated the city. Yes, she probably would like it here. "I can't wait to meet her, dear."

She flipped the journal open and began to read aloud. Most of the entries described her everyday life. Gloria thought the poor woman sounded lonely.

They were almost to the end when the journal described a frightening incident. Gloria's head jerked up. She peered at Andrea over the rim of her reading glasses. "I think we're onto something."

"Abe is furious with Hank. Hank has been involved in several run-ins with Belhaven residents. Every evening, the two of them come home from work and start arguing. I see with certainty that Hank's days here in Belhaven are numbered."

The journal had one more entry. *"Last evening, Abe and Hank got into a horrible fight. They began to shove each other. I feared the worst and retreated to our bedroom where I shut myself in. Still, I could hear the shouting from my room. I decided to try to calm them*

*down. When I reached the door, the arguing
ceased and it grew silent. Hours later, Abe
came to our bed. I was still awake.*

*I asked him if all was well. He told me that
Hank had left and that he wouldn't be returning.*

*I was greatly relieved with this news and
today things are much calmer."*

Andrea's mouth dropped open. "You think he
killed him in the heat of the argument and then
buried his body in the shed?" she whispered.

Gloria closed the journal and absentmindedly
ran a finger along the spine. That made the most
sense. But Abe was long gone. Who had moved
the body from the shed to the dumpster? Did
Abe have an accomplice? She couldn't wait to get
the lab results.

Gloria pulled herself from the chair. "This
journal belongs to you," she told Andrea. She
nodded to the bookshelf nearby. "I'll put it over
here." She made her way over to the bookcase

and spied a small gap on the middle shelf. She slid several books to the side to make room. The book was halfway in when it caught on something.

Gloria slid the book back out and reached her hand into the small space. On the side of the wooden bookcase was a small catch. She turned to Andrea. "There's something back here."

"Really?" Andrea wandered over to the light switch and turned it on.

Gloria slid her glasses up and peered in. The bump looked like some sort of button. She pulled several of the books out and set them on a lower shelf.

Yes. It was definitely some sort of button, she decided. She turned to Andrea, who was now standing directly behind her. "What is this?"

Andrea shrugged her shoulders. "I haven't the slightest idea."

Gloria pressed the small button. The girls jumped back as a scraping sound echoed in the room. Like the sound of concrete when it rubs against metal.

The bookcase began to swing back.

Andrea's mouth dropped open when the bookcase stopped to reveal a room. "Another secret room," she whispered.

There was a light switch just inside the secret room. Gloria flipped the switch and the room flooded with bright light.

Andrea took a step forward. "What the heck?"

The windowless room was rectangular in shape. Lining the walls were paintings. Paintings in every size. Big. Small. Even a few that were round. Above each of the larger paintings was a picture light.

The girls stepped inside and studied the walls. *So this was where the famous Sofia Masson paintings had been hidden!* Gloria thought.

254

Andrea ran her hand along a gilded frame. "These must be worth a small fortune," she gushed.

"Hello?" Someone out in the hallway was calling. The girls quickly stepped out of the room. Andrea pressed the button and the door scraped shut. It closed seconds before the construction supervisor stepped into the library. "There you are. I have a question."

Andrea followed the man back into the sunroom while Gloria put the books back in place.

When Andrea returned, she said exactly what Gloria herself was thinking. "We should keep quiet about this. At least for now - until we find out who put the body in the dumpster."

Gloria jumped back in detective mode. Was Hank Johnson after Sofia's paintings? Could that be the reason for Abe and Hank's heated arguments? Was someone else lurking nearby, searching for the paintings? They needed to flush out whoever the person was and Gloria had an idea!

"I have a plan," she whispered in a low voice. Gloria pointed to the door. The girls walked out front and over to Gloria's car, out of earshot. "You need to pretend you're leaving town for a couple days – or at least overnight. That way, whoever is still out there will try to get back into the house, thinking that you're gone."

Andrea nodded. Gloria went on. "You can stay at my place. We'll hide your car in the barn. We can do a stakeout of the house and hopefully catch the person red-handed."

She had a sneaking suspicion that whatever was in the locked room in the basement was what the intruder was after – or maybe it was the paintings. If they gave the person the perfect opportunity to come back, maybe, just maybe, they would have the intruder. Possibly even a killer.

"We will have Dot and Ruth spread the word that you made an emergency trip back to New York because your father was in the hospital or something." She waved her hand. "We can work out the details later."

With a rough plan in place, Gloria hopped in the car and headed to town. She'd need a little help on this one and she knew exactly who to ask. The Garden Girls!

Chapter 14

When she got to Dot's place, she called an emergency meeting that included all the girls: Dot, Ruth, Margaret and Lucy. She needed some back up to pull this thing off.

Ruth was the last to arrive. She ran a weary hand through her hair as she approached the group standing in the back of the restaurant. "This better be important," she warned. "Good thing Kenny was around to watch the post office for me." Kenny was the rural mail carrier and Ruth's right hand man.

The group of girls headed out to the picnic table, which was behind the restaurant, while Ray and Dot's employee, Holly, covered the front.

Dot balanced a tray of iced teas and a pile of baked goods as she made her way through the rear screen door. She set them in front of Lucy, who promptly reached for a chocolate frosted cupcake and lemon bar.

Gloria eyed the lemon bar in Lucy's hand. All the sleuthing was making Gloria hungry. She grabbed a lemon bar and set it on the napkin in front of her. "I need some help," she announced.

She filled the girls in on the details of the investigation so far. The people she'd talked to: Eleanor Whittaker, Doc Decker and his wife, Martha, George and Maxine Ford. She summed it up. "I think maybe Abe Johnson argued with his brother and there was some sort of accident or maybe even murder."

She went on. "The only problem is, someone is hoping to get rid of the body and it sure ain't Abe, which leads me to believe there was another party involved in the murder. I mean, why else would the person go to all the trouble of sneaking back onto the property to dispose of the body?"

The girls nodded in agreement. There certainly seemed to be more to the story.

Gloria thought of something else. She pulled the old black and white photo from her purse. The one with the men standing in front of the old mill. She handed the picture to Ruth who studied the picture and passed it to Lucy. "Doc Decker told me he thought that was my mother."

The girls had all grown up in Belhaven and they all knew Gloria's mother, Esther. They passed the picture around the table.

Margaret frowned. "Are you sure this is your mother?" The photo was grainy. She wasn't convinced it was Esther. None of them seemed convinced it was Esther.

Gloria glanced at the photo. "Doc said there was some sort of skirmish when Mother worked at the mill. She didn't work there long. Dad made her quit," Gloria told them.

Lucy nibbled the chocolate on top of her cupcake. "Sounds like no one liked the stepbrother, Hank." She peeled back the paper and took a bite. "This is delicious," she told Dot.

Gloria tucked the old photo back in the corner of her purse and snapped it shut. "We need to flush out the person stalking Andrea's place. I think there's something inside her house they want and I think it's in the basement in that locked room."

She told them how Andrea had said that someone had been in her house not long ago. "They came in through the back door, which is close to the basement door. And the basement cellar doors were unlocked."

The girls nodded. They would do whatever they could to help!

"Andrea and I are going to do a stakeout." Gloria looked at Ruth and Dot. "You two need to spread the word that Andrea is leaving town tomorrow and that she won't be home for a day or two." Which was the truth. She wouldn't be home. She'd be at Gloria's!

Gossip was Ruth's middle name. "I've got it covered!" she said.

She looked at Lucy. "I'll need a lookout. Someone waiting nearby in a car that can follow the person or persons after they leave the house."

Margaret reached for a cheese Danish. "What about me?"

Gloria shrugged. She didn't have a real plan for Margaret.

A thought suddenly occurred to her. "There are two roads that lead away from the house. The alley out back and the main road out front." She pointed to Lucy. "One of you cover the alley, the other the main road. That way, no matter what direction they take, we'll have them covered."

Margaret nodded. "We need walkie-talkies," she said. "Remember the ones I took to the mountains? We can use those."

With a plan in place to flush out the perpetrator the following night, they headed back inside. Gloria called Andrea on her way home and laid out the plan.

Gloria's heart pounded as she thought about the stakeout. She hoped they weren't just wasting their time and she hoped that Paul would get back with her in the morning with the autopsy results.

Gloria was wound tighter than a top the rest of the afternoon. When the phone rang, she nearly jumped out of her skin. It was her sister, Liz.

"Frances is driving me crazy," she moaned. "This missing Milt thing has taken over all of Dreamwood. Why, do you know she's put up missing posters all over town?"

Gloria grinned. She could picture poor Milt's face plastered on every telephone pole and grocery store bulletin board from here to Grand Rapids!

Liz went on. "She asked if you could come by and do a little snooping around. I told her I'd run it by you."

Gloria looked out the window. It was almost dark. She wasn't good at night driving any more. Plus, she was tired. It had been a long day. A long couple of days with the boys. "I'm knee deep in Andrea's dilemma at the moment. Tell Frances to hang tight. It might be a day or two until I can get over there."

Liz groaned. "Oh, you're killing me!" She sighed. "I'll let her know. At least it's something."

Before she hung up, she asked Liz what she thought had happened to him. "Honestly, I don't know. He isn't one to just up and disappear."

Unlike Liz, herself, who loved to cause a stir by taking off without telling people where she was going...

After they hung up, Gloria popped a frozen dinner in the microwave and sat down at the table. She'd been so busy, she hadn't even had a chance to read the daily news. She unfolded the paper and slipped her reading glasses on. There, on the cover, was a picture of Andrea's painting. She peered down to read the caption:

"Painting by famous artist, Sofia Masson, is discovered during recent renovations of an old Belhaven home."

The article went on to tell how the owner discovered the painting inside a dumpster, taped to the back of a sheet of paneling. It gave Andrea's name *AND* her address.

Gloria wasn't sure if this was good news or bad news. It would certainly get the attention of whoever had been lurking around Andrea's place. It was time to get the stakeout under way!

Chapter 15

Gloria was up early the next morning. She'd spent the night tossing and turning as she plotted out the plan for later that night. She also thought about the old black and white photo. The more she thought about it, the more convinced she was that the woman in the picture was not her mother!

She was sipping a cup of coffee, catching up on local news when Andrea called. "What time do you want me to come over and hide out?"

Gloria glanced at the clock. It was still early. Something dawned on her. Something she hadn't considered yet. "What are we going to do with Brutus?"

"Got that covered. Margaret stopped by a few minutes ago. She told me she'd keep Brutus until I get back."

Gloria let out a sigh of relief. It wasn't that she didn't want to keep Brutus at the farm. She just wasn't quite sure how Mally would react. The two dogs had met briefly but there was a big difference between a quick visit and having another dog invade Mally's turf!

Before they hung up, Andrea told her she'd pack an overnight bag and head out. Gloria made her way out to the barn to open the double doors. She unlocked the padlock and shoved the doors open. She peered in. The tractor took up a good deal of room but Gloria was certain there was plenty of room for Andrea's car to pull in beside it.

She was still in the barn when Andrea pulled in the drive. Gloria quickly motioned for her to pull forward and into the empty spot.

Andrea hopped out of the car and darted out of the barn. The girls closed the door as fast as they could and shoved the lock in place. They hurried into the house and slammed the door.

Gloria pulled the kitchen shade, just to be safe. She turned to Andrea. "Did you leave the cellar doors unlocked?"

"Check." Andrea nodded. "I left the lock hanging on the door but didn't snap it down so it would look like I forgot."

Gloria gave her the thumbs up. Mally padded into the kitchen and over to Andrea. She sniffed her pant legs, then her hands. Andrea bent down to pat her head. "You smell Brutus, don't you?"

She wandered over to her doggy bed and settled in. Gloria was certain she was disappointed that Brutus wasn't with her. "Sorry, girl. Maybe next time," she told her.

Andrea pulled out a kitchen chair. Puddles sauntered into the kitchen. He eyed Andrea for a moment before leaping into her lap. He curled up in a ball and settled in.

Gloria scowled at the traitor. "Maybe you should get a cat."

Andrea stroked his soft fur. Puddles began to purr like a lawn mower in high gear. "I've been thinking about it," she admitted. "Not sure how Brutus will react to a cat."

The afternoon seemed to drag on. Gloria was used to coming and going as she pleased.

At least she was able to make a few trips outside with Mally. She was certain Andrea must be going stir crazy. Although she seemed to be handling it quite well.

Andrea played on her laptop. She played with Puddles, who loved every second of it. It was obvious he adored her as much as she adored him.

Gloria thawed the chicken pot pie she'd made a few weeks back and whipped up a batch of corn muffins to go with it. After the girls had eaten, they changed into their stakeout clothes. Black slacks, black shirts, sturdy black shoes. Ones that they could run in, if necessary.

The group had agreed to rendezvous at 9:00 p.m. The plan was for Andrea and Gloria to park Annabelle at Lucy's place. Lucy would drop them off in the alley, behind the house, and then Lucy would find a place to park on the side street. Somewhere out of sight. Margaret would be waiting nearby - at the other end of the alley.

Lucy's porch light was on when they pulled into the drive. Gloria glanced around as they slid out of the car. She hoped no one would drive by and see Andrea. That was one of the downfalls of living in such a small town! Everyone knew everyone and, thanks to Dot and Ruth, Gloria was certain that 99% of the residents now thought Andrea was out-of-town on a family emergency!

Lucy opened the door. The girls stepped inside the house and Gloria quickly switched off the yard light. "I hope no one noticed Andrea," Gloria said.

Lucy's face drooped. "I'm sorry, Gloria. I didn't even think about that." Lucy was becoming a pretty good detective. She wasn't quite there yet, but she was close.

"It's okay. Don't worry about it."

Her face brightened as she reached behind her and grabbed a wrapped present off the stand. She thrust it in Gloria's hand. "Merry Christmas!"

Gloria frowned as she looked down at the package. "It's not even close to the holidays."

Lucy nodded. "I know. I was going to give you this as your Christmas gift but I figured you could use it tonight."

Gloria slid into the chair and set the box on the table in front of her. She untied the bow and peeled the tape off both ends. She turned it over and pulled the last piece of tape off before lifting the box. Printed on the front were the words: *True Grit Night Vision Monocular.*

Gloria opened the box and pulled out what looked like part telescope, part binoculars. "Oh, I get it. Monocular. Like half a binocular."

She turned it over in her hand. "Lucy, this looks expensive," she scolded her.

Lucy waved her hand. "Naw! I got a great deal on one of those middle-of-the-night infomercials. You know, buy one, get one free. I'm giving the other one to Bill for Christmas. Except he has to wait for his," she explained.

Gloria closed one eye and held the monocular up to the other. "This thing is cool! Shut off the light."

Lucy killed the lights and Gloria moved the monocular around the room. "Wow! This really works. Except you both look like little green women!"

"I know, right?" Lucy giggled. "I couldn't resist. I already checked it out."

Gloria handed it to Andrea. "Take a look."

Andrea held it to her eye and surveyed the room. "Wow. This is pretty cool!" She pulled it from her eye and handed the monocular back to Gloria.

Lucy switched on the light and grabbed the walkie-talkies. She handed one to Gloria. "I stopped by Margaret's place earlier and picked these up. We set them on a frequency so we can hear each other."

Gloria smiled. She was proud of the girls. They were getting this sleuthing business down pat!

The drive to Andrea's was quick. Lucy pulled her yellow jeep down the rutted alley and dropped Gloria and Andrea off at the edge of the of the property line, right in front of the low bushes. "This place looks familiar," Lucy commented wryly.

Gloria winked at Lucy. It looked familiar because it wasn't long ago that Lucy and Gloria had staked out the old house, which at the time was vacant. Andrea hadn't purchased it yet.

Gloria gathered up the walkie-talkie and monocular and slid out of the passenger seat. Andrea slid out of the back seat and quietly closed the door. They watched as Lucy stepped on the gas and bounced off down the alley, in search of a hiding spot close by.

The girls tiptoed over to the edge of the shrubbery and vaulted through a small opening. They crouched down and crept over to the corner, taking cover behind a large bush.

Gloria dropped to her knees. She handed the walkie-talkie to Andrea. "I'm putting you in charge of communications."

She lifted the monocular to her eye and adjusted the lens. When she had a clear view of the house, she handed it to Andrea. "Have a look."

Andrea squinted through the lens. "That is so cool. I think I'm going to get Brian one of these," she decided. She handed it back to Gloria and sat down on the grass. "I've never spied on my own house before."

Gloria chuckled. The irony of the situation wasn't lost on either of them.

They sat there quietly for several long moments and watched as the stars came out. It was a beautiful night. Gloria didn't stargaze often. She was usually in bed; sound asleep before the 11:00 news.

"So how long do we wait?" Andrea whispered.

Gloria shrugged. She was more of a fly-by-the-seat-of-your-pants kind of detective. "I'm not sure yet," she answered truthfully. She prayed they weren't wasting their time.

They sat there for a bit longer when something caught Gloria's attention. It was a small movement over on the other side of the rose garden. She whacked Andrea's arm. "Did you see that?" she mumbled under her breath.

Andrea shook her head. Gloria lifted the monocular to her eye. "Someone's out there." She followed the figure. The person was tall and walked with a bit of a hunch. She watched as the figure bent down and grabbed hold of the cellar door. "They're going for the cellar door."

Andrea squinted her eyes. She couldn't see much of anything. It was too dark, even with the stars out.

Gloria gave her a blow-by-blow. "Yep! They took the lock off the door and set it aside." She sucked in a breath. Her armpits began to sweat. "Now they're opening the cellar door. They switched on a flashlight and.....they're inside!"

Andrea started to get up. "We should go confront them."

Gloria grabbed her arm and pulled her back down. "No! What if they have a weapon?" she whispered. "Radio the girls and tell them to get ready. Someone's in the basement."

Andrea nodded. She'd completely forgotten her assignment!

She turned her back and faced the bushes before pressing the button on the radio. "Buttercup and Mrs. Trace, do you copy?"

Gloria's head whipped around. *"Buttercup and Mrs. Trace?"*

Andrea shrugged. "Undercover names I just thought up. Buttercup for Lucy's yellow jeep and Mrs. Trace since Margaret lives on Lake Terrace," she explained.

The radio crackled. "We hear you," Buttercup replied.

"Yeah! Our chicken has come home to roost," Andrea answered cryptically.

Gloria almost burst out laughing. She started to say something when a light caught her attention. Whoever had been in the basement was coming back out.

Gloria fixed her monocular on the movement. She could see something in their right hand. Something large. "They're carrying something and it's square."

Andrea could make out the outline as they closed the cellar door and put the lock back on top. "Stand by," Andrea mumbled into the radio.

Gloria's heart started to pound as the person abruptly turned and headed right towards them. The girls ducked behind the bush. Gloria squeezed her eyes shut and prayed they wouldn't be discovered.

They held their breath and waited several long moments, afraid to even blink. Finally, Gloria peeked around the edge and let out a sigh of relief. The person had turned and eased out around side of the shrubs, heading for the alley.

Andrea pressed the button on the radio. "They're headed your way, Buttercup, carrying what looks like a suitcase or briefcase."

"10-4" came the brief reply.

Andrea wasn't done. "Mrs. Trace, do you copy?"

"10-4"

"Rendezvous at green 10. Stat."

Gloria rolled her eyes. Andrea was really getting into this!

Apparently, Margaret figured out what "green 10 stat" meant as headlights bounced down the alley and came to an abrupt halt near the edge of the hedge.

Gloria and Andrea climbed through the bushes and into the car. Gloria leaned over the front seat. "If we hurry, maybe we can catch up with Lucy."

They caught up with Lucy as she was heading down main street, coming from the opposite direction. The two vehicles stopped at the corner. They rolled down the windows.

Lucy stuck her head out the window. "You're never going to believe who that was!"

"...and then they tossed the suitcase in the trash can out by the curb and walked back in the house like nobody's business."

The girls had parked in the empty lot in front of the post office. "We have to go get the suitcase," Gloria decided.

Lucy's eyebrows shot up. "What if we get caught?"

"We're not going to." Gloria didn't feel quite as confident as she hoped she sounded. "Look, I'll get it out."

Andrea touched Gloria's arm. "I can't let you take that risk," she told her.

But Gloria was firm. This was her investigation. Her reputation was at stake! She turned to Margaret. "Drop me off at the end of the street and pick me up at the other end."

Margaret gave her the thumbs up. "Gotcha."

The two climbed in the SUV. Lucy and Andrea watched them go. "I wish I had some popcorn. Or better yet, a Snickers," Lucy decided.

Margaret rolled to a stop. Gloria slid out of the passenger seat and crouched low as she slunk down the dark road toward her destination. Thankfully, there weren't many street lights in the area.

When she got to the trash bin, she glanced up. A lone light shone brightly through the upstairs window.

She carefully lifted the lid and reached inside, praying that her hand touched the suitcase and not some slimy, rotting food. Her hand made contact with a hard surface. She ran her hand along the top until she could feel a handle. She gave the suitcase a quick yank as she pulled it out. With suitcase in hand, she quietly eased the lid shut.

Gloria glanced around furtively and then darted down the road. She could barely make out Margaret's SUV parked at the end of the street. She picked up the pace when she thought she heard footsteps coming up behind her. Thankfully, she made it to the SUV without incident. She jerked the door open and slid inside.

Margaret stepped on the gas and peeled out as they made the short drive back to the post office parking lot. Lucy and Andrea were inside the jeep. Lucy rolled down the window. She popped a banana chip in her mouth. "Didja' get it?"

Gloria rolled down her window. She wrinkled her nose at Lucy "*What on earth?* Are you *eating?*"

"Banana chip." Lucy glanced down at the bag of trail mix in her lap. "The chocolate pieces are already gone," she explained.

Gloria shook her head and lifted the case. "Got it! Let's head back to Lucy's place."

Margaret followed behind Lucy and Andrea as they drove out of town. Gloria rubbed the palm of her hand across the surface. She could tell it was old – unlike the fancy new suitcases. The ones with spinning wheels and long handles.

Lucy's porch light was off. The girls crept up the steps and made their way inside. When they got inside the kitchen, Gloria set the old suitcase on the kitchen table. In the bright light, they could see several badly worn spots, where the shiny brown coating had rubbed off. The hinges on the back had rusted. The handle, although scuffed and pitted, was intact.

Gloria flipped open the latches on each side and took a quick breath. She looked around the table. "Ready for this?" She didn't wait for an answer as she lifted the lid.

The girls leaned forward and peered inside.

Lying on top was a plaid, button-down shirt. Gloria plucked it from the case and carefully placed it inside the lid. Beneath that was a pair of bib overalls. She set those on top of the shirt.

Inside the case were a few more items: a couple more shirts, similar to the button-down, along with a second pair of overalls. At the very bottom was a shave kit, right next to a pair of dark, leather work boots.

"You think this stuff belongs to Hank Johnson?" Andrea wrinkled her nose.

Gloria shrugged her shoulders. She couldn't be a 100% certain.

She placed the overalls and shirts back inside the case and put her hand on top of the lid. She started to pull the lid closed when she noticed a small, square tag in the center. She pulled her glasses from her purse and slipped them on. She leaned in for a closer inspection. She sucked in a breath and read the name on the tag: "Hank Johnson."

Chapter 16

Gloria plucked her cell phone from her purse and dialed Paul's number. He was on duty but she knew he'd still answer if he could, which he did.

"Hello?"

Gloria got right to the point. "I'm with Andrea, Lucy and Margaret. We have Hank Johnson's suitcase and we know who put the body in the dumpster," she blurted out.

Paul leaned back in his chair and stared at the wall of his office. "I wish I could say I'm surprised," he replied. "How'd you figure it out?" He didn't give her a chance to answer. "No. Don't answer that. Where are you? I'll be right over."

Lucy fixed a pot of coffee while they waited for Paul to arrive. She put into words what each of them was thinking. "I wonder if they're going to make an arrest tonight."

Twenty minutes later, Paul's car pulled into the drive. Gloria opened the back door and he slipped inside. His eyes settled on the suitcase, still sitting on top of the kitchen table. He made his way over to the table and flicked the clasps open, then lifted the lid. He inspected the contents before turning his gaze to his girlfriend. "I can't wait to find out what happened."

Gloria started the story with their plot to flush out the culprit. The others chimed in one-by-one with various details.

Gloria summed it up. "So when Doc Decker dropped the suitcase into the trash can in front of his house, I went back for it," Gloria concluded.

"Did he see you?"

She shook her head. "I don't think so, but I can't be certain."

"That doesn't make him the killer," she argued. "Maybe just an accessory to the crime." She didn't want to believe Doc Decker was a murderer.

"I just talked to the lab. The autopsy took longer than they thought but it's finally complete. When we know the cause of death, we'll go from there." He grabbed the suitcase and headed for the door. Gloria walked him to his car.

He opened the passenger side door and dropped the suitcase on top of the seat before he turned back around. "What am I going to do with you?" He didn't wait for an answer as he leaned over and kissed her lips. "I don't know how you do it. Somehow you always manage to be right in the thick of things," he told her.

After he left, the girls gathered around the kitchen table for a few minutes to discuss the evening's adventure. Now that things had settled down, Andrea decided to mention the secret room in the library that she and Gloria had discovered and what that might mean. "I need someone to come take a look at the paintings. I'm afraid to move them."

Gloria looked over at Margaret. "Do you think your art dealer friend would make a trip to Belhaven?" she asked.

Margaret promised to call her contact in the morning. Lucy walked the group out to their vehicles. She was sad to see them go. The adventure had been fun. She frowned at the thought that Doc Decker might be a killer.

Margaret left first.

Lucy walked over to the passenger side of Gloria's car and held it open for Andrea. "Are you going home tonight?"

Andrea shook her head. "If Gloria doesn't mind, I'll stay with her just in case Doc Decker decides to come back..."

Gloria nodded. "We need to be careful, especially if he decides to check on the suitcase and finds it missing."

Lucy watched as Andrea climbed into the passenger seat. "I heard you have a new roommate coming to live with you."

Andrea nodded. "Yep! Alice will be here tomorrow. I'm picking her up at the airport."

Lucy grabbed the edge of the door to push it closed. "I can't wait to meet her." She glanced back at mercury light on the side of her outbuilding. The bright light illuminated the crates, still stacked against the wall. "Hey! I heard you have a handgun at home and you do some target practice."

Andrea nodded. "I'm getting to be a pretty fair shot," she said.

Lucy grinned. "What do you think about taking out a few small explosives? You know - blow up a potato or pumpkin for fun..."

"Lucy Carlson!" Gloria had settled into the driver's seat. She slapped her hand on her forehead.

Andrea grinned.

Lucy winked at Andrea. "We'll talk later."

Gloria shook her head as she started the car and backed out of the drive.

Back at Gloria's house, the girls chatted for a few minutes. Both of them were too wound up to sleep right away.

Andrea pulled a glass from the cupboard and filled it with tap water. She took a small sip. "You want to stop by tomorrow afternoon when I get back from the airport?"

Gloria nodded. "Absolutely! I can't wait to meet Alice!"

Gloria gave Andrea a quick hug before Mally and she wandered off to bed. Puddles, the turncoat, slunk into Andrea's room to curl up on her bed.

Surprisingly enough, Gloria fell asleep within seconds: her dreams filled with monoculars and exploding pumpkins.

Andrea was already awake and had fixed a pot of coffee by the time Gloria rolled out of bed. She was nibbling on a piece of peanut butter toast and reading the morning paper when Gloria shuffled into the kitchen.

Andrea grinned when she caught a glimpse of Gloria's hair standing up on end. Gloria caught the look. "What? What's wrong?" She automatically put her hand to her head and tried to pat down the pointed tips.

"You should spike your hair more often," Andrea advised. "It makes you look…"

"Trendy?" Gloria prompted.

Andrea nodded. "Something like that." She folded the paper and took her coffee cup to the sink to wash it. "I should get going. I need to make a pit stop at the house before I head to the airport. Oh, and I have to stop by Margaret's place to pick up Brutus."

Gloria poured a cup of coffee and walked Andrea to the barn to retrieve her car. She waved to her young friend as she pulled out of the barn and headed down the drive.

She wandered back into the house and glanced at the phone as she headed to the shower. She was anxious for Paul's call and the autopsy results.

By the time she was showered and dressed, she was growing impatient. She glanced at the clock in the kitchen. Surely he must have the results by now! She reached for the wall phone when her cell phone rang.

"I was getting ready to call you," she told him.

"I have the results back on the burlap bag and nail the boys found in Andrea's shed."

"And?"

"The body belonged to Hank Johnson. He died from some sort of blunt force trauma. He had a skull fracture and a broken rib. And that nail that you found?"

"Yes?" Gloria sucked in a breath.

"It had pierced the back of his skull."

Gloria walked over to the kitchen window and stared out. "That's what killed him?"

"The medical examiner isn't sure. The skeleton is old and it's not like we have state-of-the-art equipment over here," he admitted. "It's possible that the nail didn't kill him, although it certainly could have. Or it could've been the skull fracture. The guys down at the lab have different opinions. One thinks it was the nail and the other thinks it may have been a deadly fall."

"What will happen to Doc Decker?" she asked.

"I'm running by his place here shortly," Paul told her.

Gloria hung up the phone. She called Andrea first.

Andrea juggled the cell phone against her head as she let Brutus in through the front door. She followed him inside. "Wow! Can you believe that?"

Gloria hoped the death had been an accident. She remembered the journal. "Remember what Barbara Johnson... I mean, Sofia Masson wrote in the journal? It's possible that his brother killed him during the heat of an argument and not knowing what to do, he called Doc Decker."

"But why would Doc Decker keep silent about it?"

That was a very good question. A question
that Gloria herself hoped to have answered soon.

Gloria spent the rest of the morning calling
each of the girls and relaying the autopsy results.
All of them agreed that it was possible that Abe
had killed his brother but somewhere along the
way, Doc Decker became involved.

Gloria picked up the picture of the mill and the
men out front. She slipped on her glasses and
studied the woman. The more she looked at it,
the more she was convinced that the woman in
the picture was not her mother.

She pulled the photo close and held it up to
the light. Her mother was tall. Tall like Liz. The
woman in the photo was short. Short, as in
almost the same height as Martha Decker. Doc
Decker's wife.

The kitchen chair scraped the worn linoleum
floor as Gloria slid it from under the table. She
sank into the seat and leaned forward, tapping a
fingernail on the kitchen table.

The nail in the skull. A construction nail. Gloria remembered hearing that when Doc Decker bought the drug store, he remodeled the back half so that he and Martha could live there.

She picked up the phone and called Paul. "I think Doc Decker was involved and here's why."

Paul hung up the phone. He grabbed his jacket and headed for the door. His first stop was Gloria's farm to pick up the old picture. His second stop: Doc Decker's house.

Gloria was in the garden watering what was left of her plants when Paul pulled in the drive. She was so engrossed in making sure Mally wasn't tromping over the top of the tomatoes she didn't hear him sneak up behind her. She jumped when he reached around and hugged her tight. "Oh! I didn't hear you coming!"

She shut the hose off and hung it on the hook nearby. "C'mon Mally." Paul and Mally followed Gloria up the steps and into the house. Gloria had left the photo sitting on the edge of the table.

Paul picked it up and studied the faces. He pointed to the woman on the end. "You think this is Doc's wife, Martha?"

Gloria nodded. "Doc tried to tell me it was my own mother." She wrinkled her brow. "I think he was trying to throw me off."

She followed Paul out onto the porch. "You're going there now to talk to him?"

Paul nodded.

Gloria's eyes fell on the photo. "Are you going to arrest him?"

Paul shrugged. The evidence was inconclusive. In fact, the report came back stating it was inconclusive. He would wait to see what Doc Decker had to say.

Gloria said a small prayer for Doc as she climbed the porch steps and headed back inside. The man had to be in his 80's or 90's by now. He'd never survive prison.

Chapter 17

Paul eased into the paved drive and parked to the left of the two-story home. The first thing he noticed was that there was no car in sight. The second thing he noticed was the morning newspaper, still in the drive.

He stepped up onto the porch and rang the bell. He could hear shuffling inside, just moments before the door opened wide enough for a woman's face to peer out around the edge. "Can I help you?" Her eyes traveled from his face down to his police uniform before coming to rest on his nametag.

"Officer Paul Kennedy. I'm here to have a word with Henry Decker," he told her. She swung the door open and stepped aside. "He's in the kitchen. Follow me."

Paul followed the tiny woman through the living room and into the kitchen. Henry "Doc"

Decker was at the kitchen table. Judging by the expression on his face, he was expecting the visit.

He rose from his chair and extended his hand. A small smile turned the corner of his lips. "I finally get to meet the infamous Officer Paul Kennedy," he said wryly.

Paul took his hand. The hand was old and worn, but the grip was firm and steady. Their eyes met and Paul knew Doc Decker was ready to talk. He waved to a nearby chair. "Have a seat," he told Paul.

Paul eased into the chair and rested his hands on the table in front of him. "I'm sorry to come unannounced. I was hoping you would have a few minutes to answer some questions."

Doc Decker nodded. "About Hank Johnson."

"And the night of his disappearance," Paul finished his sentence. He set the photo Gloria had given him on the kitchen table and slid it in his direction. "Have you ever seen this picture before?"

Doc picked up the picture and brought it close to his face. He slowly nodded. "I have."

Paul pointed to the woman in the photo. "Do you recognize the woman on the end?"

Doc paused. His eyes wandered to his wife, who was standing in the corner of the kitchen. His eyes never left hers. He slowly nodded. "Yes. That's my wife, Martha."

Paul leaned forward, his gaze unwavering as he studied Doc Decker's face. "Tell me about the night Hank Johnson disappeared."

Doc rubbed his chin. He took a deep breath and started to speak. "I remember that night like it was yesterday..."

Henry Decker nailed the framing board in place. He wiped his forehead with the front of his arm. The back door of what would soon be his home was wide open. It was late summer and the air was hot and humid. Even the slightest of breezes would be a welcome relief.

It was late Friday afternoon. Henry, or "Doc" as everyone called him, had worked all day in the pharmacy. Business was good. Even folks from neighboring towns like Lakeville and Fenway were coming in to shop and pick up their prescriptions. The drug store was part pharmacy and part store. The front part even had an ice cream shop, complete with an old-fashioned soda fountain.

He glanced around. The back of the place was shaping up quite nicely. It wasn't large, but he and Martha were just starting out so they didn't need much. The room boasted a small eat-in kitchen with a living room off to the side. Tucked back in the corner on the other side of the space was a bedroom and small bath.

Doc's father had been a carpenter by trade and had taught Doc everything he knew. He nodded, satisfied with the progress. *Yes, things were coming right along*, he decided.

Doc picked up his hammer and reached for a nail inside his apron when heard a small commotion coming from beyond the kitchen. He turned to see Martha shuffle through the front of the building. He noticed the red splotches on her face and could tell she'd been crying. He dropped the hammer. "What's wrong?"

"That Hank. He came back from lunch and I could tell right away he'd been drinking. He got into a fight with Matt Whittaker, right there on the office floor."

Doc took off his work apron. He pulled Martha into his arms. "You need to quit that place today. If Abe can't get rid of that scum, then you don't need to work there," he told her. "Plus, I can use you here at the drug store. Business is really picking up."

Martha nodded. Her shoulders sagged. She wanted nothing more than to quit that job!

Martha pushed back a stray hair and looked into Doc's determined eyes. "We can make ends meet, even without that job," she vowed.

Martha changed out of her good clothes and got to work, helping Doc on a few small projects around the house before they stopped for dinner. Martha had made homemade beef stew the night before and they finished eating the leftovers.

They had just finished dinner and Martha started to clear the table when they both heard a loud thumping noise. It was coming from the front of the store.

Martha eyed the front warily as Doc hustled through the door that connected their apartment to the pharmacy out front. It was dusk now, but he could still see clear as a bell through the front store window. Out front on the sidewalk were two men and they were shoving each other.

His expression grew grim when he realized one of the men was Hank Johnson. Doc didn't recognize the other person.

He unlocked the front door and stepped out onto the sidewalk. "Boys, if you don't settle down, I'll have to call the police," he warned them.

"I'm gonna bust your chops!" Hank lunged forward.

The stranger took a swipe at Hank before he spun around and stalked off down the sidewalk.

Doc grabbed Hank's arm and pulled him in the front door of the drug store. He could smell the whiskey on his breath.

Doc talked in a low, soothing voice, which only seemed to agitate Hank. Martha came from the back to check on Doc.

When Hank caught a glimpse of Martha, he yanked his arm from Doc's grasp and staggered forward. "Well, if it isn't the breathtaking Martha Decker. You're a sight for sore eyes." Doc tried to pull him back, which enraged Hank.

Hank suddenly swung back around, his arm raised. His fist connected with Doc's face. Doc staggered under the blow. He grabbed his jaw, his eyes on fire.

Doc barreled forward and tackled Hank to the floor.

Hank was taller and thicker than Doc was.

Martha could see Hank was starting to gain the upper hand. Her eyes quickly scanned the room, searching for some sort of weapon. She darted into the back of the building and grabbed a 2x4 off the floor.

By the time she ran back into the front, the two men were rolling around on the ground.

Martha closely followed their movements. When she saw her chance, she lifted the board high above her head and brought it down on Hank's skull with as much force as she could muster. The board connected with his head. *WHACK!*

The board splintered when it made contact with the back of Hank Johnson's head. He pulled away from Doc, stunned. He stuck his hand on the back of his head. Martha glanced at the board and then the back of Hank's head. There was a nail lodged in his skull. She could see it through the thin crop of hair.

"You're trying to kill me!" Hank shouted.

Martha stood there trembling as she stared down at the broken board. Her eyes, filled with terror, met Doc's.

By the time Doc scrambled to his feet, Hank had stumbled out the front door. He disappeared down the sidewalk and into the night.

Doc rushed over to Martha, who was still gripping the splintered piece of the wood. "I hit him," she whispered.

"He deserved it," Doc replied.

Martha's shoulders shuddered. She dropped the board and stuck her hands over her face. She began to sob hysterically. Doc tried desperately to calm his young wife. Finally, when she'd calmed enough and the sobs had subsided, Doc grabbed his jacket. "I'm going to Abe's house right now," he told her. "He needs to hear our side of the story."

Martha grabbed his harm. "Don't go over there, Doc," she begged. "Something bad is going to happen."

Doc squeezed her hand. "I have to, Martha." Martha watched as Doc slid his jacket on and grabbed his keys.

He climbed into his old truck and pull out of the alley as he headed to the mansion on the hill.

Doc pulled his pick-up truck into the Johnsons drive and parked behind Abe Johnson's four-door sedan. The stately home was lit up like a Christmas tree.

For a moment, Doc almost changed his mind. He nearly backed out of the drive and headed back home. But he knew he needed to talk to Abe. To explain.

Abe would understand. He knew how his brother was.

Before he could change his mind, Doc slid out of the truck and made his way to the front door. He rapped on the metal knocker and waited. Seconds later, Abe Johnson opened the door.

The first thing Doc noticed was the wild look in the man's eyes. The second thing he noticed was that he was breathing heavily.

Abe didn't say a word. He motioned Doc inside and closed the door behind him.

Doc's eyes scanned the room before settling on a body lying on the gleaming marble floor. It was Hank Johnson and he wasn't moving.

Abe took a step closer and shook his head. "I think he's dead."

Doc sidestepped Abe and made his way over to Hank. He kneeled over the still figure and stuck two fingers on Hank's neck. Abe was right. Hank was dead.

Abe shuffled over to Doc's side. "We got into an argument. I punched him and he fell to the floor. He hit his head."

From the position of the body, Doc could clearly see the nail still in the back of Hank's skull.

"I didn't think I'd hit him that hard," Abe said.

Doc nodded. Maybe he died from the nail in his skull. Or maybe from hitting the marble floor with force. Either way, Hank Johnson was dead. Doc looked up at Abe. "What should we do?"

Abe glanced at the stairs. "Barbara locked herself in the bedroom when we started to fight." He looked back at Doc. "There's only one thing we can do. We get rid of the body," he replied.

Doc Decker finished the last sentence and looked over at Paul. "So we buried the body in the shed and hid his belongings in a locked closet in the basement."

Doc continued. "When that young woman bought the old place and started fixing it up, I worried that the body would be discovered and it would open up a whole can of worms. When I drove by the place one day and saw the dumpster, I figured it was the perfect opportunity to get rid of Hank's body."

Martha Decker spoke for the first time. "I was trying to help Doc," she explained. "I didn't mean to kill him," she whispered.

Paul nodded. "The autopsy was inconclusive. It appeared to be head trauma. Whether it was the nail that pierced his skull or the fracture from the fall, we will never know."

Martha Decker stepped over to the table. She squeezed her husband's shoulder. "Now what?"

Paul drummed his fingers on the kitchen tabletop. This was a bit of a conundrum. At the very least, Doc Decker was an accessory to the murder. At most, Martha Decker had killed Hank Johnson.

"I have to turn in the evidence." Paul stood. "If I had to guess, I would say given the length of time since the crime was committed and other information, there's a good chance you won't be charged."

Martha let out the breath she'd been holding.

"However, I can't guarantee that," Paul warned.

Doc nodded and rose to his feet. "We can always pray for the best," he said.

Chapter 18

After lunch, Gloria settled in to watch an episode of *Detective on the Side*. She had recorded it the night before while she and the girls were on the stakeout.

She was nice and comfy in her recliner and was just about to doze off when the phone rang. It was Andrea. "We're here!"

Gloria pulled the recliner upright. "I'll be right down, dear."

Gloria slipped into her sweater, grabbed her keys and headed to the car.

When Gloria pulled into the drive, she could see the top of Andrea's head. She was out in the gardens. On her way to the garden, Gloria passed the sunroom. The construction crew was gone and the sunroom complete. She cupped her hands over her eyes and peeked in the windows. It was beautiful!

Gloria followed the murmured voices over to the fountain out back. She could see more of Andrea's head now. It looked like she was talking to herself.

When Gloria rounded the side, she realized why. There, standing next to Andrea, was a short little woman. She was as big around as she was tall. Her dark hair pulled back in a tight bun. Her hands were gesturing wildly as she spoke.

When Andrea spied Gloria, she waved her over. The little woman spun around, a wide grin covering her face. Her brown eyes were warm. The corners crinkled up. She grabbed Gloria's hand.

"Ahh..Miss Gloria," she spoke in a heavy accent. "I finally meet you!"

Gloria took an immediate liking to the woman. She prided herself on being a good judge of character and this woman was the real deal!

"It's so nice to finally meet you, Alice," Gloria told her sincerely.

She nodded. "Yes! You call me Alice." Alice winked at Andrea. "My real name is Anna, but Andrea - she always call me Alice," she told her.

Andrea smiled brightly. "I almost forgot your real name is Anna." She turned to Gloria. "When I was little, I loved the TV show, The Brady Bunch. Do you remember them?"

Gloria nodded. Her kids had loved that show. *She* had loved that show.

Andrea went on. "Well, I always wanted a big family and I loved Alice, the housekeeper, so I started calling Anna – Alice."

Anna – uh, Alice - smiled. "She was lonely growing up. Her parents. They work many hours."

Alice beamed at Andrea with pride. "She a good girl. No?"

"Yes. Andrea is a very good girl," Gloria assured her.

"I cook you special dinner for taking care of her," Alice told her.

Gloria nodded. "Maybe later. I'm sure you want to get settled in."

"Yes! I no like to fly." Alice wagged her finger back and forth and frowned.

Gloria agreed. "Me either."

The three of them wandered back to the front door where Andrea gave Alice the grand tour, proudly showing Alice her home – their home - now.

While Andrea settled Alice into her room, Gloria headed to the sun porch. She opened the carved French doors and took a step down onto the gleaming Saltillo tile.

Andrea's decorating style was magnificent. The room was empty, but Gloria could envision it filled with green plants, warm, inviting furniture and cozy nooks, perfect for curling up in a comfy chair with a good book on a cold winter's day.

Andrea caught up with her a few minutes later. "So what do you think?"

"I can picture the decor in my mind," Gloria told her.

Her cell phone, which she'd tucked in her pocket, chimed. Paul had sent her a text to call. She looked up at Andrea. "I bet this is about Hank Johnson's body."

They headed to the living room and settled into the Victorian chairs perched in front of the massive fireplace.

Gloria dialed his number. When he picked up, she told him she had the speaker on so that Andrea could hear.

"Doc Decker had quite a story to tell," Paul began. When Paul finished the story, Gloria asked what he thought would happen to Doc. He told her the same thing that he told Doc and Martha. That he thought they would show some leniency considering the only thing they could prove was he was an accessory to a crime. Nothing would happen to Martha since no one was certain that the nail in Hank's skull was what killed him.

After they hung up, Gloria followed Andrea into the secret room behind the library. The one with the paintings. The girls were admiring the artwork when Alice wandered in.

"Look at these beautiful paintings," she gushed. She touched the edge of one of the frames. "It's a shame they sit in dis dark room and no one gets to enjoy them."

Gloria had to agree. It was a shame to keep them hidden away.

Andrea touched the edge of one of the larger paintings. It was one of the Eiffel Tower. "Margaret called earlier. Her friend, the art gallery owner, is coming by tomorrow to take a look at them," she explained.

Alice clapped her hands. "Oh! We have company coming? I make special lunch!"

Gloria had a thought. "Why not have a little party. You know - Garden Girls' style. A tea party with little sandwiches. Then the girls can admire the artwork, too!"

Andrea slowly nodded. "That's a wonderful idea. I can set up some tables in my new sunroom. Show off the addition plus show them the paintings."

Alice's mind was whirling. "I make every-ting from scratch," she said.

"Now, Alice. These people are not used to the spicy stuff so we'll have to go over the menu together," Andrea told her gently.

Alice waved her arms. "No. They like my cooking. I promise," she said.

Andrea and Alice walked Gloria to the door. When they opened it up, Brian was standing on the other side, his hand raised, ready to knock.

Andrea gave him a peck on the cheek. She stepped to the side so he could come in.

Alice was hanging back a bit. She'd heard Andrea mention her "friend" Brian several times. She knew he was an important part of her life. What Alice *wasn't* expecting was how utterly handsome he was.

She sidestepped Andrea. Her chubby hand flew to her chest. Her chocolate brown eyes widened. "Holy guaperas!" She grabbed his hand and brought it to her face. She rubbed the palm of his hand across her cheek and gazed into his eyes. "I am in *love!*" she declared.

Andrea giggled. "She said you were hot," she informed Brian.

Brian was eating it up. He leaned forward and kissed her cheek. "I think I just died and went to heaven!"

Alice's head twisted to the side. Her eyes narrowed. "Why you no tell me he dis good looking?" she demanded.

She turned back to her dream man. "You make beautiful babies," she decided.

Brian smiled. His eyes met Andrea's. "You hear that? We'd make beautiful babies," he teased.

It took a few minutes before Andrea was finally able to pry Alice away from Brian. But not by much. Several times Alice reached over and rubbed his arm or touched his back. Brian didn't seem to mind one iota.

Finally, she told them she was going to run into the kitchen and fix a snack. She batted her eyes at her new love. "I bring you something extra special," she promised.

Andrea watched her retreat to the kitchen. She shook her head. "I have never seen her go gaga over a male before." She tipped her head to the side. "I can see I'll have to keep an eye on you two."

She grabbed Brian's hand. "Come see the new addition." Andrea led him into the newly finished sunroom. Brian leaned back on his heels and crossed his arms. "They did a beautiful job. This looks great."

As they wandered around the room, Andrea had an idea. "What do you think about me turning this into a tea room? You know, small café tables overlooking the gardens."

Gloria slowly nodded. "You could display all of those magnificent paintings. It would be an honor in Sofia Masson's name. I think she would be thrilled to know her paintings were being admired and enjoyed."

Brian agreed. "Great idea."

Andrea tapped the side of her face. "But what should I call it? Magnolia Tea Room? Lake Terrace Tea Room?" The house was close to the lake although not technically *on* the lake - but the house was on Magnolia Street. "I like Magnolia Tea Room," she decided.

Alice stepped into the room with a tray, a teakettle and an array of bite-size treats. Gloria picked one up and inspected it. It looked like a crostini or baguette with salsa on top. "I did not have time to make anything else," Alice apologized.

"These look tasty," Gloria reassured her. She nibbled on the edge. Thankfully, it wasn't super-spicy. It was tasty though - like homemade salsa with lots of cilantro. "Delicious."

Brian took a big bite. He nodded his head. "Very good," he told her.

Alice's cheeks warmed. She nodded and turned to Andrea. "See? They like it!"

Andrea nodded. "Alice is an excellent cook. You just have to watch her. She likes to make stuff HOT."

She changed the subject. "What do you think about opening a tea room?"

Alice set the tray on the table nearby and picked up a crostini. She took a bite and gave a thumbs up. "Oh! You mean like little snacks on fancy plates?"

"Something like that," Andrea answered.

Brian devoured a few more of the bite-size morsels and downed his tea. "I have to get back to the store."

Alice's face fell. "You leave me already?"

Brian bent down and hugged her. "I'll be back," he promised.

"I need to get going, too," Gloria said. She followed Brian outside. "I'll see you tomorrow for a practice run in the tea room?"

Andrea nodded. She rubbed her hands together in glee. "I can hardly wait!"

Gloria opened the car door and slid inside. She watched as Andrea and Alice headed back indoors.

The feisty woman had Gloria's seal of approval. Alice would make a great addition to Belhaven. She had a hunch the little ball of fire was going to fit in JUST fine!

The end.

Cheddar Cheese Chicken Bake Recipe

Ingredients:
1/4 cup butter (melted)
1/2 cup all-purpose flour
1 tsp salt
1 tsp black pepper
1 tsp Italian seasoning
1 tsp garlic powder
1 egg
1 tbsp milk
1 cup shredded Cheddar cheese
1 cup Chex rice cereal (or any other crispy rice cereal)
3 skinless, boneless chicken breast halves (cut in half)

Directions:

-Preheat oven to 350 degrees
-Coat a medium baking dish with 1/4 cup melted butter
-In a bowl, mix the flour, salt, pepper, garlic powder and Italian seasoning
-In a second bowl, beat together the egg and milk
-In a third bowl, mix the cheese and cereal
-Dredge chicken pieces in the flour mixture
-Dip in the egg mixture
-Press in the cheese/cereal mixture to coat
-Arrange in the prepared baking dish.

-After all of the chicken pieces have been coated and are in the baking dish, drizzle 2 tablespoons melted butter evenly over the top.

Bake 35 minutes in the preheated oven, or until coating is golden brown and chicken juices run clear.

Serve with a side of red roasted potatoes (coated in olive oil and Italian seasoning) and baked in oven!

About The Author

Hope Callaghan is an author who loves to write Christian books, especially Christian Mystery and Cozy Mystery books. Born and raised in a small town in West Michigan, she now lives in Florida with her husband.

She is the proud mother of one daughter and a stepdaughter and stepson. When she's not doing the thing she loves best - writing books - she enjoys cooking, traveling and reading books.

Hope loves to connect with her readers!

Visit hopecallaghan.com **for information on special offers and soon-to-be-released books!**

Email: hope@hopecallaghan.com

Facebook page:
http://www.facebook.com/hopecallaghanauthor

Other Books by Author, Hope Callaghan:

DECEPTION CHRISTIAN MYSTERY SERIES:

Waves of Deception: Samantha Rite Series Book 1
Winds of Deception: Samantha Rite Series Book 2
Tides of Deception: Samantha Rite Series Book 3

GARDEN GIRLS CHRISTIAN COZY MYSTERIES SERIES:

Who Murdered Mr. Malone? Garden Girls Mystery Series Book 1
Grandkids Gone Wild: Garden Girls Mystery Series Book 2

Made in United States
Orlando, FL
01 September 2023

36624223R00200